SNOWSQUALLS AND MISSING ELVES

Lighthouse Landing Trilogy #3

*Dear Beth,
Enjoy the final book!
Hope you're not disappointed!
LD Stauth*

By LD Stauth

Copyright 2020 by LD Stauth

All rights reserved. Neither this publication nor any part of this publication may be reproduced or transmitted in any form or by any means, electronic, or mechanical, including photocopying, recording, or any information storage and retrieval system, without permission from the author.

This book is a work of fiction. Names, characters, incidents, and settings (with the exception of a few named cities or towns) are a product of the author's imagination. Any similarity between persons (living or dead), places or events is purely coincidental.

ISBN: 979-8-6974-6130-3

Dedication

He has shown you, O mortal, what is good. And what does the LORD require of you? To act justly and to love mercy and to walk humbly with your God. (Micah 6:8)

NIV-Zondervan 2011

ACKNOWLEDGMENTS

The third and final book in the *Lighthouse Landing Trilogy* is dedicated to my family, especially those suffering from Celiac Disease and gluten intolerance. As a mother and grandmother, it has been heart-wrenching to see several family members in physical pain and sometimes mental anguish—at the hands of this illness.

Remarkably, after the diagnosis came, your discipline and determination to adapt to a new, costly, diet and sacrifice foods that you loved, has been admirable.

God has been faithful in hearing our prayers and is bringing about restoration and healing.

Erin, your Celiac-friendly desserts are phenomenal, especially your date squares. The previous book, *Lighthouse Landing Lament*, and this novel, *Snowsqualls and Missing Elves* were written with you in mind. Do I see a bakery such as *Coral's Muffin Cup Café* in your future?

Remember that one day these mortal bodies will be replaced with spiritual ones.

"Listen, I tell you a mystery: We will not all sleep, but we will all be changed— in a flash, in the twinkling of an eye, at the last trumpet. For the trumpet will sound, the dead will be raised imperishable, and we will be changed. For the perishable must clothe itself with the imperishable, and the mortal with immortality." 1 Corinthians 15:51-53 (NIV-Zondervan 2011)

Love you always and forever,

Mom and Grandma,

LD Stauth

CHAPTER 1

Stall Pattern

Mesmerizing. Coral Prescott had never seen anything like it. Snowflakes flying sideways, upside down, and every which way possible—all at an incredible rate of speed. Snowsqualls. That's what they called these wild storms in the community of Lighthouse Landing. She squinted to try and make out the OPP station across the street from her bakery. Only when the squall let up in its intensity every so often could she see the front of the building. It was four o'clock in the afternoon, still daylight, but you'd hardly know it. When would the snow stop? Ten centimetres already coated the ground, according to her rough estimate, and the storm had started less than an hour ago. And to think it was only the beginning of December. Winter hadn't even officially begun.

She had to admit that this season was not her favourite. If she'd known she was moving to the snowbelt when she bought the café last April, she might have thought twice about settling in this beautiful lakeside community on the shores of Lake Huron.

Thankfully, summers were incomparable to anywhere she'd ever lived. The lake and woods drew her like a subliminal beacon. Her phone contained several pictures of incredible sunsets that she'd captured, all so remarkable that she had trouble picking out her favourite. Every few days she changed the picture on her phone's screen to reflect another gorgeous scene. The view warmed her thoughts and had her looking forward to spring.

A powerful gust of wind rattled the windows of her café, and she immediately took a step backward. The hydro lines skipped up and down, as if the storm were playing jump rope with the town. A shudder passed through her. Was it from the bitter cold seeping through the old windows or the wind itself? She suspected it was the latter. Strong winds had always terrified her. It stemmed from an episode as a young child. She'd been walking to school when a rogue gust of wind snapped a tree branch, causing it to fall directly in front of her on the sidewalk. The branch was large and full of thorns. She didn't know what type of tree it was, but even as a kid she'd understood that if it had hit her, she would have been badly injured, possibly even killed. What a horrible way to die.

Coral walked to the door, locked it, and flipped the closed sign into position. She usually stayed open until five, but doubted many people would be venturing out in this weather. Besides, she hadn't had any customers since three o'clock. As she turned off the lights and headed upstairs to her apartment, she wondered how long the storm would last. Ironically, her phone dinged as another alert popped up on her app. The weather station was forecasting up to thirty centimetres before morning. Yikes! She didn't even own a shovel. She'd have to make a trip to the local hardware store and purchase one at the next available opportunity.

Her breaths came with difficulty as she lumbered to the top of the stairs. Coral was frustrated at this backslide in her health. Since when had climbing a flight of stairs winded her this badly?

But she knew when. Ever since her abduction at the hands of the warped town pathologist, Dr. Steven James, she'd not been well. Would she ever feel herself again? Even ten weeks later, migraines from the concussion could cripple her ability to do anything but close the bakery and crash in her darkened bedroom for hours. The townspeople—also reeling from the shock of losing their mayor, a police constable, and the town coroner who was also their forensic pathologist, in one fell swoop—were very understanding. They'd also lost Ryan Burwell, the man who gave tours and maintained the lamp in the town's lighthouse. Although Ryan's arrest was not related to the murders but drug trafficking along with the mayor, she suspected the town wasn't suffering too much from his absence. Ryan was not well-liked, being the spoiled scoundrel son of a well-known and well-loved philanthropist couple Annie and Ernie Burwell. Regardless, she was happy the town was gracious in allowing their pastry chef time to recuperate.

Coral pulled open the refrigerator door and reached for the container of chili. Yesterday she'd prepared a large batch and was looking forward to enjoying another bowl. She scooped a ladleful into a dish, set it in the microwave, and hit the timer. While she waited, she leaned against the kitchen counter. Contrary to her wishes, her thoughts slipped into the same stall pattern they had since...

She swiped at the never-ending stream of tears that had started that day in the hospital and hadn't really let up. It was the beginning of December and she hadn't heard a word from Jace since he'd dropped the engagement ring and run from the room. With agony, she recalled his final words—that the ball was in her court. Coral scowled. She'd never liked tennis. In fact, was never any good at it. She didn't want to play this game. Why couldn't she rewind her life to before Luke had said that he loved her and messed everything up?

Her chest tightened until it felt as if it might explode. How could Jace love her enough to be ready to propose, then disappear from her life? He'd told Luke that he wouldn't run with his tail between his legs, but wasn't that what he'd done? She blew out a breath. Of course, part of her couldn't blame him. That unexpected kiss from Luke was most likely the cause. But truly, that wasn't her fault. She hadn't seen it coming and had been helpless to stop it in her weakened state and Luke's emotional one.

Coral reached for the box of tissues, tugged one loose, and blew her nose. She'd never had a doubt about whom she loved. Had she? It was always Jace Kelly with his expressive sea-green eyes, light brown hair, and reddish chin stubble. She loved his spunky personality, sense of humour, and the way her heart leapt when he entered a room. But Luke Degroot was so kind to her and handsome as well, with his strong athletic build, white-blond hair, and sparkling blue eyes that seemed to reach deep inside her. Not to mention, he was a good man and well-respected in the community.

Coral reached into the silverware drawer for a spoon and slammed it closed a little harder than necessary. Her dilemma on whether or not to join the Lighthouse Landing OPP had given her many sleepless nights. Because she was still a mess physically and mentally from her abduction and injuries, in the end she'd declined to apply. She would never be able to carry out the stressful job in her weakened condition. Still, her heart was in police work. Maybe one day, in the not-so-distant future, she could reapply.

It had been a few months since she was released from hospital, and Luke had come into her café almost every weekday. He was recovering well after the loss of his father from cancer. Despite his pain, Luke stopped by often to check up on her. His daily presence was comforting. At the least she'd found a good friend. As for anything else, time would make that clear. For some reason, and she couldn't put her finger on it, she'd never told Luke about Jace's engagement ring.

If Luke's mission were to win her over with kindness, it might eventually work. He'd often stop in on his lunch hour and tidy up messes left behind by customers. One time he was enjoying a coffee at one of the tables in her cafe when a delivery truck arrived with supplies. He was quick to jump up and help unload them. She was thankful for his quiet and helpful ways, especially since fatigue was part of her daily regime.

And since Jace was nowhere to be found.

Ding. Coral grabbed the bowl of chili from the microwave, stuck her spoon into it, and trudged to the living room. She'd developed a habit of sitting in front of the TV while eating. Really, she didn't have much choice without a kitchen table or even room for one.

After flipping mindlessly through the TV channels, she settled on the Shoreline News. Local reporter Scott Forester was good at his job. She enjoyed his no-nonsense accounts of local news, weather, and events. The weather was top news today—no surprise there. Scott urged caution in slowing down on the slippery roads, as reports of several weather-related accidents around town and on Highway 21 were coming in.

As Coral finished the last bite of her chili and slumped against the sofa, her cell phone buzzed. She scanned the words—a text from Luke inviting her to the town's annual Christmas parade Friday night.

It's not a date ☺. Several officers and their families are coming and, since you know a lot of them, I thought you might enjoy it.

Apparently, the local detachment made it a tradition the first Friday in December every year. Afterwards they held a party at the union hall where Santa would make an appearance and bring presents for the kids. No doubt Luke believed she really needed to get out of the house and was offering her the opportunity.

Coral started to type in a no-thank-you reply then paused with her thumbs in mid-air. She hadn't attended a Christmas parade since she was a young child. And never one in the dark and with snow. It probably would do her good to get out a little. She'd stayed sequestered with a stack of books since her accident. She typed in her acceptance and hit send before she could change her mind. Coral bit her lip. Was this a good idea? This would be the first outing with Luke since he'd declared his feelings for her that awkward day at the hospital. Would her agreement to attend give him the wrong impression? She set the phone on the coffee table. She couldn't wait for Jace forever, could she?

Her head shot up. Jace had left the ball in her court. *She* was supposed to make the first move. Why hadn't she? Was it her stubborn pride? Or was she confused as to which man had really captured her heart?

Coral rested her head against the couch cushion. Was Jace's absence pushing her toward Luke? How did she feel about the Dutch officer? So many questions, but absolutely no answers. Coral gave herself a pep talk as she rose from the couch, entered the bedroom, and slipped into her fleecy pyjamas. *It's just a Christmas parade, Coral. You're not walking down the aisle with him.*

CHAPTER 2

High-Rise Contemplations

For the umpteenth time, Jace's finger hovered over the send icon but he couldn't bring himself to do it. Something held him back. He'd told Coral to make up her mind, and he would stick to that if it killed him. And it was killing him. What was taking her so long? Had she decided on Luke? If so, the least she could do was tell Jace. This on-going silence was torture.

Jace paced in front of his expansive floor to ceiling window. It had been many long weeks and he thought he might lose his mind. Tossing the phone onto the sofa beside him, he shoved his hands in his pockets and stared outside. The view from his lofty apartment that almost dangled over Lake Ontario was incredible. But the tug on his heartstrings from Lighthouse Landing far surpassed it. And he suspected it had more to do with a certain someone than the scenic location. Although he couldn't dispute that Lighthouse Landing was unique and beautiful. Scenes flashed through his mind of walking the trail that led to the bridge overlooking the lazy river—the bridge where he'd first kissed his partner, Coral Prescott. Actually, she'd kissed him. No matter. The fireworks were the same—wildly explosive.

A memory of the two of them strolling hand-in-hand up the wooden boardwalk to enjoy the view over Lake Huron drifted through his mind. He smiled as he recalled Coral's obsession with sunsets. Despite the danger of being fired upon by a sniper at said location, Coral had insisted that they follow the mayor's fancy car into the campground. Although her daring landed them in a very precarious situation, in the end it had paid off huge. The mayor was arrested a short time later on drug trafficking.

Jace swallowed as he remembered those passionate kisses he'd stolen from Coral after a large spider had parked itself on her shoulder and she had screamed, alerting the mayor to their presence in the treeline. The kisses, meant to conceal their identities, revealed so much more, impacting him to the core of his being. He'd never felt that way before. Ever. With anyone. Where did things stand between them now? To be honest, they looked rather bleak.

How many times must he rehash that scene in Coral's hospital room? Did he delight in self-inflicted torture? Walking in on Luke kissing the woman Jace loved was akin to having the man punch him directly in the heart. Jace rubbed his chest at the thought. Suddenly his frustration peaked, and he slapped both hands on the top of his head. That's when it hit him.

What did I go and do? He recalled the words he'd fired at Luke—*If you think I'm going to run with my tail between my legs, you've got another think coming.* And then Jace had gone and done exactly that. He'd dropped the gift bag and bolted. Didn't even stay long enough to propose. His emotions had gotten the better of him, something he often suffered from.

He pressed a hand to his stomach. The mustard and pastrami on marble rye that he'd eaten for lunch swirled inside, as if he'd taken a huge drop on a fast-moving roller-coaster. Rather than fight for Coral, he'd fled. Sure, his actions appeared cowardly, and maybe to some degree they were. But the distance he'd created was designed to let Coral decide. Wasn't it? What good would a one-sided relationship be? When he was with Coral, though, it never felt one-sided. On the contrary, he thought they had something special together, that they clicked on a deep level. Not only was she beautiful on the outside but absolutely lovely on the inside. He admired how she could make him laugh yet challenge him at the same time. How was she taking his silence? Had she given up on him? Cast him aside, assuming he no longer cared? Was she seeing Luke Degroot now?

Jace's hands tightened into fists at his sides. How did Coral really feel about Luke? That was the main reason Jace had stepped back. He sensed Coral was conflicted—that she truly didn't know who she loved. After all the back-checking he'd done on the man, as far as Jace could tell Luke Degroot was a stand-up guy. Sure, he wasn't perfect. When Jace first met him, he'd thought Luke was a jerk. But that changed when Jace learned that Luke had lost his father to liver cancer a few days after the major arrests in September. The man had been under a great deal of stress at the time, so his attitude had been understandable.

The town of Lighthouse Landing still appeared to be staggering and in upheaval. Besides the mayor being arrested for trafficking a dangerous mix of heroin and fentanyl, one of the town's OPP officers, Victoria Woods, had been arrested as his accomplice. But by far the biggest news was the apprehension of Triple L, the Lighthouse Landing Lament killer. How was the town fairing after the arrest of their long-standing town coroner and forensic pathologist?

Jace contemplated an airliner as it flew directly over his high-rise apartment, heading east over Lake Ontario. The science of flying had always fascinated him. He marvelled at the thought of something so large and astronomically heavy getting off the ground in the first place. His pulse quickened as the idea charged through his brain. He could almost envision the words in big bold letters on the side of the jet. Words that said, *Go West Young Man—west to Lighthouse Landing, Ontario.*

Although a fairly new Christian, he had prayed continually about his heart-wrenching dilemma over Coral. But all he had gotten in return was silence. Was God answering him now?

Inspired, Jace sprinted to his desk and fired up his laptop. He scrolled through his emails until he found the one he was looking for. Typing in his reply, he added the attachment and hit send. He rubbed his hands together in anticipation. For the first time in several weeks, a tremulous smile crossed his face. Time would tell if he'd done the right thing. Had he really heard God directing him with imagined words on the side of a jetliner? Or was he winging it on emotion? His propensity to overreact had gotten him in many sticky situations in the past. Jace bowed his head and whispered a prayer from deep within his heart.

Lead me, God, I pray. I hope this idea was from you. Otherwise, all I may have done is messed things up further.

CHAPTER 3

Dizzy Spells and Flying Bacon

Oh! That rumbling sound hurt her head. Coral cupped both hands over her ears. What was that noise? It couldn't be morning already, could it? Squinting, she turned and reached for her cell. Eight o'clock. How had she slept so long? She must have silenced her alarm and fallen back to sleep. Now she'd have a scant amount of baking to offer her customers when she opened at nine. The head injury was really taking its toll on her. And that awful noise wasn't helping. What or who was making all that commotion?

When she slipped out of bed, an involuntary shudder charged through her as her bare feet hit the worn, chipped, ice-cold tile. After wrapping herself inside her terry robe, Coral guided her feet into a pair of blue fleecy slippers and slapped to the window. Nudging the curtain aside with a finger, she peered out. Everything was stark white and blinding as the sun reflected off the sparkling new ground cover. The weather station's prediction of a huge snowfall had been accurate after all. Although she didn't look forward to the clean-up, she had to admit that the world held a pristine beauty like she'd never witnessed before.

A dark figure, stark against the bright background, pushed a machine down her driveway. Ah. That explained the noise. Someone was snow-blowing. Judging by the man's physical size and police issue parka, she was pretty sure who that someone was. Luke, of course. Her heart warmed at the kindness of the man. She sighed. So much for rushing out to buy a shovel. Besides, given the amount of snow that had fallen, that would be about as effective as bailing out a flooded basement with a spoon.

After showering, she dressed and hurried downstairs to her café. The least she could do was get the coffee going to show her appreciation. Luke would be cold. As the brew sputtered its readiness, the snowblower puttered to a stop. Coral peeked out the window and blinked. Not only had Luke cleared her side driveway, he'd cleared the parking lot too. Of course. What was wrong with her? She certainly hadn't been thinking, had she? How would customers be able to access the café without the snow being cleared away? She'd have to be more prepared for life in this snow-belt region of Ontario.

A disconcerted feeling skittered over her as she watched Officer Degroot remove his black snowmobile mitts, slip down the hood of his parka, then pull off his police toque. When he caught her studying him through the glass, he waved. His cheeks were kissed brilliant pink from the cold, and his white-blond hair was matted down from sweat. Her smile came easy as she waved back. Was Luke Degroot slowly inching his way into a corner of her heart?

 He approached the door, brushed snow off of his pants, then stomped his feet before entering. His blue eyes sparkled like the newly-fallen snow. Despite the rosy cheeks, beads of moisture dotted his nose, and a red ridge-line from his toque rimmed his forehead. He was about the cutest thing she'd ever seen. He even smelled like a breath of fresh air. And, she had to admit, seeing Luke was a nice way to start the day. As he slipped out of his boots and jacket, Coral prepared his coffee the way he liked it.

Turning, she held the mug toward him. "Before I went to bed last night, I had plans to go out this morning and buy a shovel." Coral sniggered. "A lot of good that would have done. Thanks so much for all your hard work. I'd have never opened the café on time."

He took a large gulp and gave her a thumbs up. "Great coffee. Has anyone ever told you that your coffee surpasses them all? What's your secret?"

Coral flapped a hand at him. "Nah. It only tastes extra good because of that brisk workout you just did. Again, thank you so much. What do I owe you? I should probably ask around about hiring snow-removal help for the winter."

Luke wrapped his hands around the mug and shook his head. "You don't owe me anything. It's called being neighbourly. As for hiring snow removal help, it would be a good idea. But you may be a tad late on that. Most companies are already booked up by early October. Still, you could try. Even so, a shovel would be a good idea, at least for your steps and around the door."

Luke wandered toward her almost empty display case of gluten-free baking and stared inside. "No cinnamon buns today?" As he stuck out his lower lip in a mock pout, Coral heard a distant rumbling sound.

She angled her gaze toward the parking lot. Maybe it was the snow equipment that was clearing out the OPP parking lot across the street. When it happened again, and the sound seemed to be coming from beside her, she observed a sheepish-looking Luke. "Was that your stomach?"

Luke pressed a hand to his belly and cocked an eyebrow. "I think I worked up an appetite."

Coral pointed toward the booth. "I imagine you did. Relax and enjoy your coffee. I'll be right back."

"Okay." Luke ambled toward the bench and sat down.

Coral bounded up the stairs to her apartment a little too quickly. Grabbing the handrail at the top, she fought the wave of dizziness that assaulted her. Concussion symptoms still lingered. *No sudden movements. You know what the doctor said.* She took a deep breath, willing her tipping world to settle, then walked into her kitchen and opened the refrigerator. This was not normal procedure, cooking bacon and eggs for her customers, but considering the circumstances, she felt it was in order. After all the help Luke had given her this morning, it was the least she could do.

A package of bacon, carton of eggs, and loaf of bread in hand, she descended one step. And that was all she remembered.

"Oh my goodness, Coral. Are you okay?" A hand gently stroked her cheek. When she forced her eyelids open to the man's frantic voice, Luke's eyes were wide with alarm.

"What happened?" Coral whispered.

"You fell down the stairs. Thank God, you're okay. I was about to call for an ambulance. Don't move. I want to make sure nothing's broken."

Luke's face fluttered in and out of focus. *Nothing broken? Fell down the stairs?* When her vision finally cleared, she discovered that her body was spread awkwardly halfway down the staircase. Luke sat on the step beside her, cradling her head in the crook of one arm. He felt up and down her arms and legs with his fingers.

"Does anything hurt?" He gazed at her tenderly, eyes full of worry. "Nothing seems broken. Are you in any pain?"

She nodded. "Uh huh."

"Where?"

"My butt is throbbing."

A blush crept across Luke's face, along with a slight smile. "Oh, um, maybe we should get you to the hospital for x-rays. Could you have injured your tailbone? Do you think you hit your head? We wouldn't want that concussion to worsen any." Luke's fingers ran through her hair. "I don't feel any bumps." His gaze, inches from hers, spoke volumes of his feelings for her.

Coral's heart performed a tiny pitter-patter. Was he going to kiss her? Did she want him to? She could barely recall his first kiss in the hospital after her accident. It had come at a time when she wasn't expecting it and was in a drug-induced stupor. All she could remember from that unexpected display of affection was Jace's mortified face behind Luke. But Jace had been silent ever since. And Luke had become a good friend. Maybe a kiss from the handsome cop would help her make up her mind and decide, as Jace had insisted she do.

"You scared the life out of me, Coral. I don't know what I would have done if I had lost you." He drew in a ragged breath. Then his lips found hers. He tasted of coffee and country boy and wholesomeness. She bolted upright suddenly, and everything swayed.

Luke held onto her tightly. "I'm sorry. I'm really sorry. I said I wouldn't pressure you. I shouldn't have kissed you. That will only complicate things. But I care so deeply for you. And you had me so worried." He rambled nervously before dropping his arm from around her shoulders.

Coral's heart went out to him, and she reached for his hand. "I care deeply about you too, Luke. The kiss was nice. I'm not upset. Truth be told, I've been wondering what it would be like."

When Luke's head shot up, his eyes carried a hopeful twinkle. "You've been wondering about kissing me?"

"Oh my! Look at the mess I made." She stared at the chaos all around her. Broken eggshells scattered the steps in various locations, along with a half-open egg carton. The loaf of bread lay crushed on the landing at the bottom of the stairs.

When Luke followed her gaze, he shrugged. "Sorry about the bread. In my hurry to get to you, I stepped on it."

A tiny giggle escaped her. Was it the sight of the crushed loaf of bread? Humiliation at her clumsy fall? Or nervousness over the unexpected display of affection? "I don't know why I'm laughing. I'm terribly embarrassed."

"What's there to be embarrassed about? You fell."

"I think it was another dizzy spell. By the way, where's the bacon? I see the eggs and the bread."

"That's kind of strange. I don't see it anywhere." Luke scanned the steps and floor below. "It'll show up eventually. We'll smell it before too long." With one fell swoop, Luke picked her up in his strong arms and carried her down the remainder of the steps, careful to avoid broken egg shells and their slippery, slimy contents. Had the kiss made Luke think he could ratchet up the physical stuff? Or was it a kind, gentle act after her painful tumble?

He carried her through the café and set her down carefully on one of the couches. "You stay there and don't move. At least until the dizziness subsides. Can I get you a glass of water? Or some coffee?" He squeezed her hand.

"Water would be nice. Thank you." Coral slumped against the couch and closed her eyes—her emotions spinning as wildly as her head.

"Here you go."

She reached for the glass Luke held out and took a sip.

"You stay there. Are you sure you don't want me to call an ambulance? Or at least take you to the hospital?"

"No, I'm fine. But, um, Luke?"

"Yes?" He squatted down, both hands on her knees. "What is it?"

She squirmed on the sofa. "Can you get me a cushion for my tailbone?"

Luke popped up. "Sure thing." He scanned the room. "Where would I get one?"

"You'll need to go upstairs to my apartment. The living room is on your right at the top of the stairs. You'll find one on the couch."

"Sure thing." Luke disappeared. Seconds later, his footsteps thumped up the stairs. After about a minute, he returned, her plush aqua cushion in hand, and urged her to sit forward. He gently positioned it behind her lower back. "Is that good?"

"Yes, thank you."

He held up a finger. "Give me a few minutes."

Pots and pans clanged loudly in her café kitchen before the wonderful aroma of bacon tickled her nostrils, sending her gastric juices swirling. The swinging door to the kitchen flew open and Luke pushed through, carrying two steaming plates. He set one on the table in front of her and took a bow. "Your breakfast, my lady."

A warmth flooded her chest. She had been prepared to make breakfast for him, and now it was the other way around. Could the man be any kinder? Any more of this wonderful humanity and she'd drown in it. "I'm not sure I can eat. My stomach is a little upset. It smells really good though, so I'll try." Coral leaned forward and took a small bite of toast.

Luke dug into his food as if he hadn't eaten in days. Of course, judging from his protesting stomach before her humiliating tumble, that made sense. She didn't manage much more than her toast and a bite of bacon. "This is delicious. I guess you found the bacon. Where was it?"

He wiped his mouth on a napkin. "It landed on the decorative shelf, halfway down the steps, behind the vase of lilacs."

Coral quirked an eyebrow as she studied the man across from her. "That's crazy. It must have really gone airborne." It was obvious Luke loved her. He'd not only verbalized his feelings that day in the hospital room a few months ago but steadfastly showed them by his actions. And that kiss. Oh my.

Luke picked up their plates and disappeared into the kitchen while Coral clasped her burning cheeks. What was she to do now?

CHAPTER 4
Mysterious Santa

"How in the world can they do that?" Coral glanced at Luke as she tugged the hood of her jacket up over her lavender toque. "Won't their legs freeze?"

Luke chuckled. "They make them tough in these parts." Rows of bagpipers passed, kilts flapping in the wind, bare legs exposed. A shiver travelled her body, accompanied by goosebumps that didn't seem in any hurry to depart. According to her weather app the temperature was minus twenty-two with the windchill. Despite the frigid air, the colourful lights and festive music were making Coral's first night-time parade a magical experience.

As the hymn *Silent Night* poured from their instruments, her mind wandered back to the summer and the town's unusual yet powerfully popular tourist attraction. Every night at dusk, weather permitting, a bagpiper played his instrument from the catwalk around the top of the town's famous landmark, its proud lighthouse. To see these musicians brave the frigid winter elements was mind-boggling. She'd always loved the sound that bagpipers created. Even more so tonight, as she was entertained by not one, but several at the same time.

Coral viewed the large crowds of people that lined the downtown street on both sides. A joyful spirit hung in the air. A flatbed trailer chugged past with a banner draped along the side. The float represented the little Baptist church that she'd attended with Jace that one special Sunday. *O Holy Night* was being pumped from the speakers, and a divine aura settled over her. Coral almost wanted to fall on her knees and hear the angels' voices as the words of the song implored. The float was simple but so profound with its depiction of the night of Jesus' birth.

Sadly, after Jace had left, she'd never gone back to that little church on the hill. Not that she didn't want to. Not that she'd abandoned her faith in God. But the church held one memory too many.

Excited squeals echoed off nearby buildings as the crowd's excitement rose. Something big must be coming. Luke leaned toward her and whispered, "Santa."

"That explains it." Coral shifted her weight from one foot to the other to keep her toes from freezing. She really needed to invest in warmer winter boots. Another item on her list of survival gear in this snowy region of Ontario.

Santa's elves—young girls and boys dressed in green costumes, leotards, hats, and even green boots with bells—hurried toward each child's outstretched hand, placing a small candy cane in every palm. Parents had trouble restraining their children from racing down the road after the small green creatures.

Coral grinned at Ava, Luke's young niece, as she screeched when her daddy bent down and let her retrieve a candy cane from an elf's hand. Ava had been perched on Ben's shoulders in order to see. As the elf skipped away yelling, "Merry Christmas", Ava giggled. Luke's sister Charlene, her husband Ben, and their children, six-year-old Caleb, and three-year-old Ava, had joined them before the start of the parade.

Caleb had stood at his Uncle Luke's side right from the start of the festivities. Even now the young child held his uncle's hand, but his face carried a frown. When the bubbly elf inadvertently passed Caleb by, Luke pulled his nephew along. "Let's go, buddy." They chased the festive creature about fifteen feet down the road until they caught up with him and were rewarded with a candy cane.

Coral marvelled that such a small thing could turn a child's frown upside down. Caleb beamed as he held the candy tightly in his mitten. Oh to be a kid again and thrilled with a sweet. She could only hope that her customers were that excited over her baking.

"One for you, my lady." Luke held out a small red and white treat.

"Thank you, kind sir." Coral reached for it and tucked it into her pocket, along with filing away the info that Luke seemed good with children. One day she'd love to have a family of her own.

"Ho! Ho! Ho! Merry Christmas." The jolly words belted from the big man in red as he appeared in front of them. Screams of delight accompanied Santa's appearance as the final float with the cheerful bearded man and his bag of toys meandered past. A pair of very pretty female elves, with long blonde hair and looking exactly identical, flanked either side of Santa. They waved and blew kisses at the spectators. Coral thought they were the most adorable elves ever. They looked so much alike, they had to be twins.

When Santa caught her eye and smiled directly at her, her heart did a leap. How did Santa do that—ignite childhood excitement in a grown adult? Tonight, something magical shimmered in the air. "Who's playing Santa?" Coral kept her voice low so the children couldn't hear as she leaned toward Luke.

But Uncle Luke was busy trying to remove the plastic wrapper from Caleb's candy cane. Coral tugged on his coat-sleeve, guiding him toward her. "Who's playing Santa?" she repeated, as quietly as possible so the children wouldn't hear.

Luke's eyes narrowed. "I'm really sorry. With all this noise, I don't know what you're saying."

Coral pushed a corner of Luke's toque upward and whispered her question directly into his ear. When her lips touched his cheek as he turned, she stilled. So did he. Oops. She hadn't meant for that to happen. Ever since the stolen kiss on the stairs, she'd been on a mission to keep physical things on the down-low. "Never mind. It doesn't matter." Coral yanked his hat over his ear and searched for the float again. Santa had turned and was waving the other direction.

"I'm not sure who it is this year. Often it's Ernie Burwell. But I heard he's been ill for a few months. Kensington has been known to fill in occasionally, but keep that information quiet. It's a well-kept secret." Luke's stammered response revealed that her accidental lip-brushing had rattled him.

Way to go, Coral. Keep your lips to yourself.

She inhaled deeply and focused again on the parade. It had definitely been weird when Santa locked gazes with her. Then again, if the man in red was Kensington, it would make sense since she knew and liked him.

The parade ended and the crowd began to disperse. Ben and Charlene said their goodbyes and scooted away with the children to get them home and into bed. Luke led Coral a short distance along the main road to the reception hall—only a few buildings away from her bakery—where the local police detachment's family Christmas party was being held. She liked that almost everything was within walking distance in Lighthouse Landing. Especially since, at the moment, she was terribly cold and couldn't wait to get inside. The wind whipping off the lake dug its tentacles inside her coat, wrapping them firmly around her bones. Not to mention that it was snowing again. Coral had never been so happy to enter a warm building.

Several people were milling about, enjoying Christmas cookies as well as a variety of hot drinks. Coral hurried toward the urn marked hot chocolate. Within a few minutes, her body began to thaw, warmed by the delicious beverage. She removed her parka and draped it over the back of a chair. Her toes had finally stopped tingling—had they gotten a bit of frostbite? If so, it would be her own fault. Although she had donned the thickest pair of socks she owned, her boots were more for dressy occasions than warmth. Coral compiled a mental list in her head of things she'd need to survive winters in this snowbelt community: warmer mittens, thermal socks, sub-zero winter boots, and a snow shovel. Truthfully, she should be making a list on her phone. She'd always prided herself on a good memory, but lately the concussion had challenged that.

Luke was practically inhaling gingerbread cookies alongside Officer Rodney Newton. Those two men could sure eat. She hadn't seen that gigantic officer Newton much since the major arrests a few months ago. And that was okay with her. Truth be told, he kind of scared her. Was it Newton's military background, his formidable size, or the flinty façade he presented? The more she thought about the humungous officer, the more she realized that *scared* wasn't the correct word. Still, something about him set her nerves on edge. Thankfully, she didn't have to deal with him. But what if she followed through on her desire to one day join the Lighthouse Landing detachment? She'd have to work with Newton then. Something to seriously consider. Perhaps, if she got to know him better, she'd feel differently. But she'd have to wait for another posting, as she'd informed Kensington several weeks ago that she was not going to apply. The position was probably filled by now. Constant headaches would cripple her ability to handle the highly stressful and demanding job at this point in her life. Even though she believed that things happened for a reason, it rankled her that she couldn't return to police work. Coral sighed. Perhaps there was a reason she was unaware of?

Kensington approached, his pretty wife in tow. Her shoulder-length hair was a most unusual colour—a cross between silver and mauve. Cora wondered if it was natural or tinted. Along with her petite stature, she reminded Coral of a violet—a pretty flower that her mom had grown in their gardens in Vancouver.

The woman extended a hand. "Hi. You must be Coral, our famous bakery chef. I'm Sylvia. Nice to meet you. I've heard great things about you." Her handshake was delicate, yet firm at the same time. It carried a subliminal 'I might be small but don't mess with me' message.

"Nice to make your acquaintance. And I don't know what you heard, but I'm sure it was exaggerated."

Coral smiled as she flapped a hand around the room. "This is very nice."

Sylvia's eyes lit up. "Glad you like it. I look forward to putting this event together every year. With the help of other officers' wives, we organize and decorate. The children get so excited when Santa enters the room. I live for their responses. Speaking of that, here he comes."

She lived for their responses? Sylvia must really love children. Come to think of it, Coral didn't believe the sergeant had ever mentioned having children of his own. And if Santa were approaching, it couldn't be Kensington playing the part, because he was standing right beside his wife.

The pair of cute teenage elves that had been positioned with Santa on the float skipped into the room, more candy canes in hand—very large candy canes. In the darkness of the parade, Coral thought they were younger from their petite builds and shorter statures. But now she judged them to be on the older edge of their teenage years.

Sylvia shook her head. "Oh no. When I told Gabby and Evangeline to buy more candy, I didn't expect foot-long treats. The parents are going to take me to task over this."

A boisterous "Ho! Ho! Ho!" floated across the room. Santa's magnanimous greeting announced his presence, much to the children's glee. There was something very comforting about Santa's voice that brought a smile to Coral's face. She must really be missing her childhood. Santa dragged a big red bag behind him as he lumbered toward a chair covered in a maroon cloth. A superbly decorated Christmas tree to his left had many expertly-wrapped gifts stacked neatly underneath. Why was Santa dragging a bag, which appeared empty, when all the gifts were under the tree? Tradition?

One of the twin elves, whose name-tag said Evangeline, held up a list. Odd. Wasn't it supposed to be Santa that checked the list? No matter. Children's names were called, and one by one they hurried forward to receive their gifts. The twin elves worked in tandem. Evangeline Elf called out a name and Gabby Elf searched for the present and handed it to the happy child. Most of the kids politely thanked Santa and scurried away to join their parents.

One young boy charged the stage when he heard his name. In his excitement, he tripped and fell face-first into the pile of presents. Gabby, in her haste to get out of the way, stumbled backward into the tree. The tree wobbled precariously, but somehow remained upright as Evangeline reached out a hand to right it. The tree-topper, a gold metal star, teetered and wobbled before it fell from its perch, landing directly on Santa's head. A collective gasp trickled across the room as Santa sat in what appeared to be stunned silence.

Glittering like the Star of Bethlehem, it swayed for a split second before tipping off of his head and toppling to the floor. Santa reached up, rubbed his head, and groaned, "Oh! Oh! Oh!" causing laughter to trickle across the room. Silly Santa. Who was playing the part since it obviously wasn't Kensington? Not that it really mattered, but something about the North Pole iconic figure intrigued her.

Elf Evangeline helped the toddler to his feet. The child, unaware of the ruckus he'd created, grabbed his gift, and raced toward his parents. A few moments later, after all the gifts had been dispersed, Santa whispered to one of the elves.

Gabby Elf scanned the crowd. "Is there a Coral in the room?"

What? Her heart stumbled and sputtered. Santa had a gift for her? She glanced around. There must be a young girl here named Coral. Her cheeks warmed with foolish embarrassment at the rise of child-like excitement inside. When silence followed, Luke reached for her hand and held it high. "She's right here."

Oh boy. When all eyes locked onto hers, Coral wanted to lift the edge of the dangling red tablecloth—which matched the shade of her cheeks—and disappear under the dessert table.

"Come on, Miss Coral. Don't be shy." Evangeline crooked a finger at her.

"If he makes me sit on his lap, I'll slap him," Coral mumbled as she approached the jolly bearded man. Luke chuckled behind her as she staggered forward on wobbly legs. She wasn't one to like all eyes on her, but that's exactly what was happening. The room had grown silent, even the noisy toddlers had stilled.

She wiped her clammy hands on the sides of her pants as she stopped in front of the man. She'd rather be in hot pursuit of a felon than centred out like this. Awkward. Santa reached into the bag, withdrew a small, shiny, foil-wrapped box, and held it out to her. When their eyes connected, her heart sped up like a herd of charging rhinos.

"Thank you, Santa," Coral stammered. She snatched the gift then turned and fled to the security of Luke's side.

Sylvia walked to the stage. As the sergeant's wife thanked everyone for coming and wished them all a very Merry Christmas, Coral couldn't keep her eyes off the man in red. What had just transpired between them?

Santa was rubbing his head. Did he have a headache from that star that struck him? A ludicrous desire to see if he was okay came over her. What in the world was wrong with her? Was she crushing on Santa?

Santa got up from his chair, clutched his bag, and clomped toward the exit in his sloppy black boots. My, but Santa was thin. He needed to eat more cookies. Perhaps she should offer him some of her baking. The room grew quieter as families dispersed.

Luke slipped his arms into his coat. "I've never known Santa to do that. In fact, after asking around, no one seems to know who's playing Santa this year. Are you going to open that gift?"

"I think I'll wait until I get home." Coral set the pretty box on one of the tables and reached for her parka.

A few minutes later, the pair clomped through a swirling snowsquall toward Coral's place. "The weather is nuts in Lighthouse Landing. How do you live here?" Coral complained as she hung onto her hood with one hand, and clutched the present with the other.

"You get used to it." Luke held open the outer storm door of her apartment.

A fleeting thought passed through Coral's mind as she dug into her pocket for her key. Had Luke arranged this? His blank expression told her no. She'd come to know Luke well enough and he was usually very readable. But maybe, just this once, he'd tricked her and surprised her with a gift. Coral shook her head. That would be a weird way to do it. "Goodnight, Luke. Thanks for inviting me. It was fun. There's something very magical about a nighttime Christmas parade."

"You're welcome." Luke's gaze lingered on her lips. "And there's something very magical about being with you."

Coral gulped. "Goodnight, Luke" she muttered, quickly ducked inside, and closed the door.

Her fingers trembled as she reached for the pretty gift. Was that nerves from Luke's compliment or a reaction to the bitter cold? She pulled off the green bow and peeled back the shiny gold foil. The substantial weight of the box set her anxieties to rest. If the gift were from Luke, at least it didn't appear to be a ring—unless he'd slipped a rock into the package to throw her off. It didn't make sense that Luke would give her a Christmas gift in such an unusual manner. Why not present it personally, instead of making a scene at the local police force's annual Christmas party? From everything she knew about the man, he wouldn't operate like that. How would she feel if Luke *had* proposed? She couldn't answer that question.

Wrapping paper torn off, she lifted the lid on the box and withdrew the hefty gift. A snow globe? No wonder the box had felt heavy. She peered inside the glass and gasped, immediately clasping the object to her chest. Only one person would know the significance.

Her heart beat erratically, and she felt short of breath. Eyes misting over, she held the gift out and studied it again. She could barely see the bridge through tears—the one in Sleepy Acres campground that held so many precious memories.

Unbelievable! Jace Kelly was Santa.

Now it all made sense. The odd feelings coursing through her when Santa waved to her from the float and as he handed her the gift. And the inane notion to hurl herself onto Santa's lap and hug him like a long-lost friend, despite her words to Luke a moment earlier about slapping Santa if he tried to make her do so. An incredulous desire to giggle came over her. Jace was in town. And he'd reached out to her. He'd said the ball was in her court, but he'd changed the game plan. Fingers still shaking, she reached for her cell and texted him.

C. You're the skinniest Santa I've ever seen.
J. What can I say? The last few months have been tough.
C. I'm speechless. The gift is so perfect.

J. Can I see you tomorrow?

C. Yes.

J. Need a hot shower. Caught a chill. That costume wasn't warm enough. Have a headache too, after that clonking with the metal tree topper. Can we meet for breakfast at your café?

C. Yes.

J. Goodnight.

C. Goodnight.

Hope surged through her as she donned her pyjamas, snuggled under her covers, reached for the snow globe, and studied it again. It had a black marble base with white swirls throughout. When she flipped it upside down, snow drifted over the bridge and river. Wait. Words were etched in the marble—*The Bridge to Happiness.* Joy galloped through her. How had she missed that important message? This was the spot where they had shared their first kiss. So did that mean what she thought it might?

A knob protruded from the back of the globe. Coral twisted it until it could wind no farther. A familiar song drifted out. Her heart swelled to the music of *Holy, Holy, Holy, Lord God Almighty.* That was the hymn that she and Jace had sung together their one and only week in church. And he had remembered.

Overcome with emotion, her lower lip quivered. Could this really be happening? Was his gift saying what she thought it might? Then her joy quickly deflated like a tire from a porcupine's quills. How in the world would she ever tell him?

CHAPTER 5

Bittersweet Reunion

It was mid morning and no sign of Jace. Had he undergone a change of heart about seeing her? After she'd set a tray of chocolate-chunk peanut-butter cookies in the oven, Coral's phone buzzed. She fished the device from her apron pocket, studied the screen, and relaxed. Jace asked her to put the coffee on and he would be right over. After assuring him she'd have a fresh pot waiting, she took a moment to check her appearance in the mirror over the sink. A perplexing thought charged through her brain. Odd how, with Luke, she never really cared what she looked like. Of course he was here almost every day, sometimes popping by unexpectedly more than once in a day.

After readying the coffee, she stared outside. It was still snowing but seemed to be reducing in intensity. The area had received another huge dump of the sparkly stuff overnight. No wonder she hadn't had a customer yet. No sign of Luke clearing out her parking lot and driveway today either. Maybe he was tied up responding to accidents in the storm, most likely the reason for the unsettling sirens throughout the night. What would Luke think when he found out that Jace had played the role of Santa? Or of the interesting gift she'd received from him? An uneasiness settled over her. Luke wouldn't be happy.

Coral folded her arms across her chest as she contemplated the glistening white expanse. What was wrong with her? Why couldn't she remember to buy that desperately needed shovel? Remnants of the concussion still reeked havoc with her mind. Regardless, she needed to hop on board and deal with winters in this snowy lakeside community. To be fair, she had contacted several snow-removal companies, and all were booked.

Her heart skipped a beat at the sight of the man who had crossed the street and was now trudging through knee-high snowdrifts in her parking lot. Had Jace come from the OPP station?

Perhaps he had stopped by to say hi to Kensington. The two of them did share an easy bond. Jace's cheeks were crimson from the cold. Coupled with a black parka and toque, he stood out like a penguin on an iceberg. Then again, he'd always stood out since the first day she'd met him.

What did his gift truly mean? Was it as significant as she thought it might be? The words etched in the marble carried mountains of promise. In fact, when she stopped and thought about it, the whole situation was unusual. If she didn't have the evidence in hand this morning, she might actually have thought she'd dreamed the whole thing.

A gust of blustery air blew in with the serious-looking detective. He'd barely crossed the threshold when, after one look into those piercing emerald eyes, she fell into his open arms, snowy coat, and all. Didn't even notice his icy-cold cheek resting on her head. How long had she dreamed of this reunion? In his arms she felt as if she'd finally come home. Crazy, because this *was* her home.

"Those were the hardest weeks I've ever spent in my entire life." His breath hitched and his voice broke. He tipped her chin up to face him. "When days went by without any contact from you, I couldn't sleep. I couldn't eat. I don't know how to explain it any other way, except that I was homesick—homesick for you, Coral."

Could someone's heart actually burst? She marvelled at his words that mirrored her thoughts only seconds ago. Deep inside existed a mysterious, mindboggling connection. Gloved hands clutched the sides of her face before he dipped his head. His lips were deliciously warm despite his outdoor trek. Heat coursed through her like a power surge on a hydro line. Too soon, he broke the kiss and pulled her against him, wrapping her securely in his arms. "Oh, how I've missed you, Coral. I'm sorry, so sorry, for how I left things between us. Can you forgive me?"

She wrapped her hands around his neck. "I'm sorry too. I should have contacted you long ago. I don't know why I waited but I ..."

He kissed her forehead, then each eyelid. Her head swam, dizzy with elation, until he reached up and removed her hands from around his neck. Puzzled, she watched him pull off his gloves and toque, unzip his parka, and slip it on a hook by the door. "We have lots to discuss, but I'm in desperate need of a coffee. Not to mention, there's a major incident unfolding at the moment. I can't stay long."

"A major incident? I'm confused. Do you have to leave for Toronto?"

Jace strode to the coffee pot and poured himself a drink. He took a large gulp and nodded toward the seating area. "Let's talk."

Something felt off. She wobbled toward the booth, feeling as though her joy was about to nose-dive from a precarious cliff.

"I don't even know where to begin." He clutched his mug. "I have so much to tell you." His countenance grew serious. Shadowy half-moons hung below his eyes, as if he hadn't slept all night. Coral perched on the edge of the bench seat, twisting her hands in her lap.

"Considering the gravity of the unfolding situation, do you mind if we temporarily delay the talk about us? I have so much more to tell you but …"

What in the world was going on? The mention of an unfolding incident had certainly piqued Coral's curiosity. "Sure. What situation? Has there been a terrorist threat in the Toronto area?"

"Gabby and Evangeline are missing."

"Who?" Confusion charged through her brain as she tried to process the information he'd relayed. "Are you talking about the twin elves that accompanied you last night?"

Worry lines etched his forehead as he nodded.

"What happened?"

"We don't know if they got lost in the snowstorm or if it's something else. Their parents reported them missing about one a.m."

"Oh no."

"Apparently, they still live at home, on a farm about twenty minutes northeast of town. At first, it was assumed they had slipped off the road or gotten stuck in a snowdrift. But if that was the case, they would have called and let their family know."

Coral sat up straighter in her chair and instantly bit her bottom lip against the pain. Waves of discomfort radiated through her lower back while her coccyx complained at the movement. For the most part the tailbone was healing well, but occasionally it reminded her of her recent fall. Hopefully Jace didn't notice. There were more important things to worry about right now. "I assume that didn't happen?"

Jace shook his head.

"Can they not be located by the tracker on their mobile devices?"

"Yes and no. Their phones are pinging a location on Concession Road 7, about five minutes from home. There's been no communication since they left the Christmas party last night around eleven. They'd stayed to help Kensington and his wife clean up the place, then they were supposedly driving straight home."

"I'm confused. If their phones are there, why couldn't you locate them?"

"We tried, but it was impossible to get to them. We went out shortly after the call came in but were hampered by the fierce storm. Visibility was so poor we had to call the search off. It was too dangerous to be on the roads. Even snowploughs were pulled off. We hadn't even made it to Concession 7."

Coral shook her head. "The storms around here are out of this world. I would have thought blizzards like that only existed in the Arctic. Still, why wouldn't the girls call for help? It doesn't add up."

"Unless they're both badly injured and unable to call, in which case it makes me sick that we couldn't get to them. I have to say that I'm getting really odd vibes from this whole thing."

"Maybe they decided to walk to the nearest farm?"

"And leave their phones in the car? And not let anyone know what was going on?" Jace shook his head.

Coral sighed. "True."

"Apparently, the twins are conscientious, hard-working young women who often volunteer their time for many worthy causes. Both work long hours on the family chicken farm. According to the parents, their daughters were about to spread their wings, pardon the pun, and rent an apartment together in town."

Coral cocked an eyebrow. "Sounds like they're responsible. How old are they?"

"Twenty-two."

"I never would have guessed. I thought they were teens. Is that what all the sirens were about last night?"

Jace headed to the coffee pot for a refill. "Yes, as well as several accidents. We're waiting for this snow to finally let up and the roads to be ploughed before we resume our search. The parking lot at my hotel hasn't even been cleared. That's why I walked here."

Coral stood and walked over to stand beside him. "What do you mean you've been searching? You talk like you're on the case. Did Kensington cajole you into helping or did you volunteer? And how did you come to play Santa?"

Jace blew out a breath. "Like I mentioned, we have lots to talk about. Technically I'm not on the case but helping as you suggested. The Santa part came about as a fluke. But come January first, I'll be assuming Kensington's role when he retires—sergeant of the Lighthouse Landing OPP Detachment."

Coral reached for a mug just as a beeping sound came from the kitchen. The mug slipped from her hands and crashed to the floor. Her mouth fell open, but no sound came out. He'd applied for the job he knew she wanted? How could he do that to her?

Beep. Beep. Beep.

"Is that your fire alarm going off?" He sniffed the air.

"It's the timer for my cookies, but it could just as easily be a fire alarm." Her eyes flashed. "I'm smoking mad at your betrayal. You know I wanted that position. What are you trying to prove?" Impulsively, she pressed a palm to his chest and shoved.

Jace stumbled backward, coffee from the mug slopping over onto his hand. "Calm down." He reached for a napkin and swiped at the drips. "I'm not trying to prove anything. Kensington contacted *me* and asked if I was interested. I was surprised when he told me that you hadn't applied. I figured that you'd changed your mind for some reason and decided to stay with the bakery. I thought this was the answer to *us*. Apparently, it wasn't." He set down his mug, his eyes darkening from their usual tranquil sea-green to a stormy, gale-tossed ocean.

Bells continued to ding, and a faint burning smell hung in the air.

Jace straightened abruptly, as if someone had poked him hard between the shoulder blades. His jaw tightened. "I have a set of twins to find. Way more important than sparring with you at the moment. Until you figure out what you want, I'm done. No more changing my game plan. Perhaps Luke is the man for you after all." He stormed toward the exit.

Her vision blurred. "Fine. Get out." She swung toward the door, about to point to it, and froze. Luke stood there, twirling his toque in his hands, an awkward expression on his face.

"You get out too. Now! Both of you." Whirling, she disappeared through her swinging door to salvage what was left of her smoking, blackened cookies.

CHAPTER 6

Snakes and Dates

That woman is driving me nuts! Jace squelched the desire to yell those words at the top of his lungs into the frosty air. Truthfully, he didn't have the energy after his adrenaline-filled clomp through the parking lot. He had believed himself to be in top physical shape, but his exercise workouts didn't usually involve deep snow. He stopped at the edge of the road to catch his breath.

How could the tender, emotion-filled reunion between the two of them take such a sour turn only minutes later? No matter what he did, he couldn't seem to make Coral happy. Maybe a relationship with her wasn't meant to be, and Luke had actually captured her heart. Perhaps Coral had been waiting for the right time to tell Jace that very thing. But that kiss. There was no mistaking the explosion. At least on his end.

He stared at the empty road, which mirrored his barren heart. If she truly loved him, why did she let several long weeks of silence dangle between them? He distinctly remembered telling her that the ball was in her court. As far as he was concerned, the ring spoke highly of his feelings. Couldn't she see that? Why did he go and change the game plan? A vision of the jetliner flying over his apartment came to mind. He'd thought God was directing him to return to Lighthouse Landing and claim the woman he loved. Had he heard God wrong? Yet … he had been so sure.

He studied the precinct as he approached. Had he done the right thing when he accepted the position in Lighthouse Landing? Jace entered the police station and stomped the snow from his boots as Sergeant Kensington strolled into the lobby.

"You look as bad as I feel." Kensington squeezed the bridge of his nose and propped a shoulder against the door frame. "I feel the start of a cold coming on. What's your excuse?"

He grunted as he removed his coat and hung it on the hook by the door. "I'd rather not talk about it. Sorry about your cold."

"Okay, suit yourself. Update on the Fillmore twins in the conference room now." Kensington shoved away from the doorway and strode down the hallway.

Relieved the sergeant hadn't pressed any further, Jace slipped out of his boots and into his work shoes before following the distinguished and highly respected man.

Jace nodded at several familiar faces as he located an empty chair at the far end of the long table in the conference room. He swallowed the nervous bulge in his throat as he considered the humungous change waiting for him in a few short weeks. Could he do it? Lead with fairness and integrity, yet garner respect as Kensington had?

Heaven forbid that anyone get wind of his horrible nickname in Toronto—Catastrophe Kelly. He'd like to think he'd come a long way from his former, nasty, combative self in the last year. To think he'd blamed all the incompetent officers who'd only lasted a day or two as his partner. How was it that he couldn't see the problem had been him?

Truthfully, he owed his transformation to God, even though Coral had been instrumental in pushing him to get help. At first he had balked at Coral's conditions—conditions that left him a mess for almost a year. Balked was not really an accurate word. More like vehemently rebelled. To be truthful, he'd been furious. She had demanded that he settle things with his father and find God, or the two of them could never be together. Two almost insurmountable tasks, yet here he was. He could never have done it without God's help. The hostility against his dad was gone, but the pain of rejection still lingered. To be completely honest, he still struggled from time to time. Slowly, though, he was re-building that relationship with his father.

Jace slumped in his chair. What did Coral want from him? He was a new man, free from bitterness and loved by God, and still they couldn't seem to make things work between them. Maybe he'd waited too long, and Luke had slithered right in and stolen his place in Coral's heart. Jace scanned the room. The snake was missing. Of course, because he was with Coral. Why hadn't Luke left when

Coral ordered them both to go? If he had, then why wasn't he in attendance at this important briefing? To be fair, Jace didn't know that it had been called either unless … he dug into his pocket for his cell phone. The message had come through, and he hadn't heard it. Probably around the time he was basking in that mind-blowing kiss.

He felt like trudging back across the street, hauling Big Dutch out of the café by the ear, and dragging him into the meeting. When Jace became sergeant at the start of the New Year, strict attendance would be adhered to or disciplinary action would swiftly follow. Jace shot to his feet. "Why isn't Degroot here?"

Every eye in the place turned his direction. No sooner had those words crossed his lips than Luke appeared in the doorway, a large white pastry box in hand.

"Here you go, Serg. I grabbed a variety of several different types of baked goods." He set the box in front of Kensington. "I even managed to get a whopper of a date."

Jace grimaced at Luke's incomprehensible remark. Coral's choice was now very obvious. But when Luke's comment was not accompanied by a gloating glare, Jace was confused. If the shoe was on the other foot, Jace would have dug the comment in and slapped a smug grin on his adversary at the same time. He winced. Perhaps he hadn't quite conquered the nasty part of himself during his character transformation. Apparently, he had a long way to go yet.

Kensington rubbed his hands together and grinned. "Coral told me she'd save the juiciest and largest date square for me. Best news I've had all day." He quirked an eyebrow at Jace. "I commissioned Degroot to purchase treats for the meeting. You have a problem with that?"

"Um, no sir."

While Luke slipped out of his coat, Jace slunk down on his chair, feeling more like the snake that he'd just accused Luke of being. *Get a grip, Kelly. Luke was referring to a dessert date, not a date-date, you idiot.* If he planned to fill Kensington's shoes in another month, he needed to leave his personal problems at home. And judging by Luke's stellar performance review and volunteer community service that Jace had been able to read over since he'd be assuming Kensington's position, the Dutch officer had more scruples in his baby toe than Jace had in his entire body. Perhaps Luke wasn't a serpent after all and would ultimately make Coral happier. Maybe it was time to step back and let the better man win.

Kensington removed his coveted pastry from the box, set it on a napkin, and passed the remainder around the room. "There's a full pot of coffee on the counter. Feel free to get up and help yourself at any time." The sergeant took a bite of his dessert before setting it down and brushing crumbs from his lips with the back of his hand. "County ploughs are out now, clearing roads. Once we receive the okay, we'll resume our search for Gabby and Evangeline. To update, sadly there has still been no contact from the twins. Ed and Brenda Fillmore are beside themselves with worry."

Officer Sam Jenkins raised a hand. "What kind of car were the girls driving, sir?"

"A white 2012 Toyota Corolla."

"Seriously?" The gigantic officer who sat beside Jenkins snorted. "Who would be brainless enough to own a white car in the snowbelt region of Ontario?"

Jace cringed at Officer Rodney Newton's insensitive comment. Two women were missing. Why criticize their choice of vehicle colour at a time like this? Jace figured he was going to have his hands full with this cocky ex-military character. A few months ago, Newton, who had been a new employee at the time, had taken a verbal swipe at Kensington's age and mental capabilities after he overheard the sergeant offer Coral, a mere bakery chef, Kensington's job when he retired. Sure, Newton hadn't known about Coral's past history in police work, but that was no excuse for his disrespect. Kensington had bristled then set the man straight. But it appeared Newton hadn't changed much. Perhaps he was pushing the boundaries since Kensington would be gone in a few weeks. *Not on my watch.*

Kensington pressed his lips into a flat line and glared at the man. "I drive a white vehicle. You calling me brainless, Officer?"

The entire room fell silent, all eyes glued on Newton.

"Never sir."

"Finding a white car in all that snow might make our job a little more difficult but not impossible. If you feel you're not up to the task, Marie Nesbit is having trouble with her combative neighbour again. This time she caught the man backing his truck over his own blue box, tossing it onto her front lawn, and stealing hers. I need to send someone out to appease her and make sure the weasel gets her a new one." Kensington fired the challenge at the sassy officer.

"How hard can it be to find a small white car in several feet of snow?" Newton shrugged, his lips twisting into a cockeyed smirk.

"That's what I thought." Kensington reached for his mug as snickers bounced around the room. After taking a swig, he set it down and approached the white board where a map of the county was taped. A large yellow mark highlighted Concession 7 between Highway 21 and the small town of Armstrong where the Fillmores lived. "The women's cell phones last pinged halfway down the concession. For some reason, the GPS signals have stopped transmitting their location. Officer Miller informed me that it may due to the extreme cold, especially if the phones were exposed to these frigid temps all night long, or else the batteries have died." Kensington used his highlighter to mark an X at the spot on the map. "According to their parents, this is the route the girls normally take to get home from Lighthouse Landing, first heading North on 21, then east on 7. I don't need to stress how imperative it is that we find that car and the twins. If they are injured or have been exposed to those temps all night, well, enough said."

"Degroot, you and Detective Kelly will search Concession 7 driving west to east. Carlisle, you're with me. We'll check the same road, driving east to west. The ditches are deep, and it'll take lots of eyes to complete a thorough search. Newton, you're on the Nesbit incident. Officer Miller has the details of the ongoing neighbour feud and the location. Perhaps, she'll even accompany you if you ask kindly enough."

Amusement coursed through Jace. Ha. Kensington was going to teach this cocky ex-military to guard his tongue. Good for the sergeant.

Newton stared at his superior. Jace could almost see the fumes coming out of his nose, like a bull ready to charge. To his credit, Newton kept silent. But Jace had other things on his mind. How in the world could he work with Degroot? Especially after this morning's incident. How much did Big Dutch actually hear of the exchange between Jace and Coral? Jace cast a glance at the tall, buff, blond officer. As soon as the two of them made eye contact, Luke glanced away and studied the screen on his mobile device. Was he texting Coral? *Enough.* Jace sighed, forcing himself to curtail his rampant thoughts. Hadn't he reprimanded himself a few minutes ago about leaving his personal problems out of the work place?

He shifted his attention to Miller, the young and petite female officer. How was it he'd never met her before? Was she a new recruit? He'd have to ask Kensington about her later. The cheeky grin she had hurled at Newton revealed a feistiness that made up for her size. It appeared she could handle the ex-military man. And Carlisle—Jace had forgotten his first name but not his appearance. He was a rather rotund fifty-something man with thick, grey curls.

"For those remaining behind, Scott Forester of *Shoreline News* has somehow gotten wind of our missing twins. Not sure how, but if he calls again, or shows up requesting info, don't give him any. Not yet. Let's wait and see what we find. We'll know within the next hour or two if something more sinister than a car slipping off the road in a blinding snowstorm has occurred. Let's hope and pray the women couldn't make calls because of a dead wi-fi zone or some other logical explanation and we find them alive and well, stuck in a snowy ditch. Dismissed."

Kensington turned to leave then pivoted back around. "Oh, perhaps this isn't the best time to announce this, but since we're waiting for the final all-clear from the snow removal crew, I'd like you to meet your new sergeant starting January 1st. Detective Jace Kelly, can you stand please?"

Jace got to his feet. Officer Luke Degroot flashed him a belligerent glare. Okay, the man was human after all and wasn't too pleased with the change ahead. Or was it more personal—the fact that his challenger for Coral's affections was moving to town? Kelly forced himself to tamp down the gloat that came with that thought.

"Detective Kelly comes with glowing qualifications from the Toronto OPP Homicide Division. Many of you know him from a few months ago when he was instrumental in capturing Triple L, or the infamous Lighthouse Landing Lament Killer. He happens to be in the area for a few days, and since he's already resigned his position in the big TO, volunteered to help on the case. Let's all give the man a hearty, small-town welcome."

Clapping broke out, with several congratulations rippling around the table in his direction. He waited for the applause to die down and raised a palm. Everyone looked his way. "Thank you for that warm welcome. I already know most of you, but some I don't." He nodded at Officer Miller. "I look forward to this new opportunity and hope that I can fill the big shoes I'm following. Thank you." He plunked onto his chair.

Chatter resumed. Kensington excused himself to take a phone call on his cell. Officer Miller appeared at his side, extending a hand. "Hi, I don't believe we've met. I'm Andrea."

Jace clasped her hand. "Nice to meet you. Are you new? I don't remember you from the Lament Killer case."

"No, not new. I've been employed here eight years. I was off on sick leave over the time of the murders." She shook her head. "Unbelievable in our small town. And to think it was our esteemed coroner. I wonder how Officer Woods is doing. I warned Victoria about getting involved with that shady, full-of-himself mayor, but she didn't listen. Now, I've lost my good friend to a possible several-year prison sentence."

Jace studied the woman. He didn't mean to stare, but it was hard not to. While she spoke, her hands flew through the air in dramatic motion, and the rate at which she talked astounded him. He almost needed a speed translator if there was such a thing. Could she even breathe between words?

Her huge hazel eyes, shadowed beneath a canopy of long, thick lashes, were alive with animation. A light sprinkling of cinnamon-coloured freckles scattered across her nose and cheekbones, giving her a youthful appearance. Rich fiery-red hair settled on her shoulders in gentle waves. Although her build was petite, she exuded strength and vitality. When she placed a hand on his shoulder and left it there a little longer than necessary, he rose.

"Nice to meet you. I need coffee." He headed for the pot on the counter. His thoughts swirled at Officer Miller's actions. Maybe she was trying overly hard to be friendly and make a good impression, but in case it was more than that, he'd nip any flirtatious overtures in the bud.

Kelly gulped the tasty brew and studied the officers that would be under his command. As he scanned the room, he felt a pair of eyes trained on him. Officer Andrea Miller. When their eyes connected, a smile—laced with hint of suggestiveness—crossed her face. Yes, she was very pretty, he couldn't deny that. But not only would a relationship with one of his officers be inappropriate, he wasn't the least bit interested. His heart was already taken. The coffee soured in his mouth as a weight crushed his chest. What if he couldn't resolve the issues between him and Coral?

"Roads are cleared. Let's go." Kensington's booming voice dragged him back to reality. *Dear God, help us find these girls alive and well.* He dumped his remaining coffee in the sink and hurried from the room, careful to avoid any further contact with Officer Miller.

CHAPTER 7

Abominable Snowman

Jace couldn't believe his eyes. He'd never in his entire life seen snowbanks this high. How in the world would they ever find a small white car? Newton had made a valid point after all, despite his snide comment about the girls being brainless to purchase one. Searching for them in mountains of snow would make their task that much more difficult.

Officer Luke Degroot drove the squad car, which was fine with Jace. It freed him up to concentrate his search out the passenger window instead of manoeuvring slippery, icy roads. Luke had way more experience in this type of weather than he did. The car was cloaked with a blanket of awkwardness. It appeared that neither of them wanted to be the first to speak. At some point they'd have to lay aside their personal differences and come to a place where they could be civil to each other and work together. Especially today.

Finally, they reached Concession 7. Degroot made a right turn and inched the cruiser along while Jace scanned the ditch. If it was deep, like Kensington stated, it was difficult to tell with the amount of white stuff everywhere.

Thankfully, there wasn't any traffic on the road, which made their job a lot easier. The storm had finally passed, and the sun shone brightly on the freshly fallen snow. Jace squinted at the blinding white expanse. The view was so intense it made his eyes water. He pinched the bridge of his nose and blinked several times.

"You can borrow my extra pair of sunglasses if you like. They're in the glove box."

The tension in the air was finally cut with Degroot's offer. Again, Jace felt small next to the man. Despite the fact that Luke was most likely worried and upset by Jace's reappearance, he had made the first move at breeching the friction with the kind offer. Jace was certain that Luke recalled that painful scene in the hospital room as much as he did—the scene where Luke vowed to fight for Coral. Jace almost smacked himself on the forehead with the palm of his hand. What in the world was wrong with him today? *Focus on the job, Kelly, not on personal issues.*

"I think I'll take you up on that." Jace started to reach for the glove box handle then froze. "Wait a minute. Stop. I see something." Jace held up a palm toward the windshield.

Degroot slowed the vehicle and brought it to a full stop. Jace opened the door and set one foot on the road. Raising a hand to shield his eyes from the glare, his pulse quickened at the red reflection of a taillight. Relief charged through him as his eyes adjusted enough to discern a white car lodged at about a seventy-five degree angle in the ditch a dozen feet away. Jace ducked inside the squad car, excitement edging his voice. "I think we found them. Can you let Kensington know? I'm going to check it out."

Jace clomped down the road in his knee-high boots until he was directly opposite the car. He'd had to borrow a pair of winter footwear from Kensington, as he certainly hadn't been prepared for this weather when he'd decided to play Santa and surprise Coral. He peered down at the vehicle. The back driver's side door was wide open. Odd. It probably meant that the girls had climbed out through the back, since the front doors were barricaded in snow. The car didn't appear to be damaged, which was a good sign. Hopefully, that meant no injuries.

Trudging down the steep, narrow incline was difficult. He was almost to the car when he fell, slipping the remaining few feet and slamming into the driver's side front tire. Oomph. After picking himself up, he peered into the open back door. Snow had blown inside, covering the floormats and leaving a white coating in various other locations. No sign of the women. Partially buried under snow, two purses lay on the floor of the vehicle, a large pink one and a smaller black one. Packages of candy canes lay helter-skelter all over the interior, most likely extras from the Christmas party that had slid off the backseat when the car tipped.

The sweet smell of chocolate tickled his nose. A brown liquid had frozen onto the dashboard and part of the windshield in a sloppy, star-like pattern. A paper cup also lay on its side on the dash. One of the girls must have taken a carryout cup of hot chocolate from the party and the contents dumped during the ditch dive.

Kelly's brow wrinkled. If the twins had decided to go for help, why would they leave their purses behind and the door wide open? A quick check through their handbags and no cell phones were found. Maybe the devices were somewhere else in the car, but a cursory scan didn't reveal them—odd since the GPS had pinged them here until a few hours ago. Jace climbed in and did a more thorough search, checking under the seats, in cup holders, the glove box, and the console. Strange. The cell phones were nowhere to be found.

Painstakingly, he made his way out of the car and the steep ditch. If only he had something to hold onto, like a sapling or two. He ended up practically crawling on his hands and knees. Man, that was one sharp-angled slope. He slipped several times, face-planting once, before he finally reached the road. Jace opened the passenger door of the squad car and leaned in. "The car is empty and doesn't appear damaged. No sign of the girls. And get this—they left their purses behind. I couldn't locate their cells, but the car is a mess after tipping on that angle."

Degroot's mouth hitched up at one corner. "Kensington's on his way. This may not be the time for jokes, but forgive me, you look like the abominable snowman. Were you trying to make snow angels?"

Jace rolled his eyes. "Very funny. I'd like to see you manage that vertical climb without falling at least once."

Degroot shrugged and slid him a sideways grin. "Piece of cake. Don't forget I grew up in the snowbelt."

Jace wrestled with the man's amicable behaviour. Degroot appeared to be a stand-up guy. He didn't remember him being this nice a few months ago, although it was possible that his judgment had been clouded at the time. Regardless, he could understand why Coral might be attracted to him. As Kelly brushed at the snow on his clothing, despair about the whole situation hung over him. With a nickname like Catastrophe Kelly what chance did he have against this man?

Red flashing lights approached, distracting him from his downward spiral. Back to the extremely important case at hand. And rightly so. The police car containing Kensington and Carlisle pulled in front of them on their side of the road. Degroot stepped from their car. He left the cruiser lights flashing to warn drivers of their presence. All four officers met on the road between vehicles and stared into the ravine.

"Sir, there was no sign of the women and their purses are still in the car." Jace knocked a clump of snow from his pants. "I didn't see their cell phones either."

Kensington's countenance darkened. "I have a bad feeling about this. Did the women decide to leave the vehicle to go for help and become disoriented? If so, that could mean they're lost somewhere in a field. In those frigid temps last night, chances for their survival would be slim to none. Or—I hate to even think it—were they abducted by a so-called Good Samaritan who stopped to help? But what would be the odds of that happening out here in the middle of nowhere during a raging blizzard?"

Jace pressed his lips together, biting back his retort. He didn't want to answer that question. Over his years in police work, he'd seen the odds defied more often than he could count.

"Degroot, call for a tow truck and we'll get this to the station where we'll do a more thorough search inside. Perhaps even fingerprint it. I'm not liking the looks of this. One. Little. Bit." Kensington waved a hand toward Carlisle. "You stay with Degroot, and Kelly, you'll accompany me. The Fillmores are a few minutes down the road. We need to tell them what we've found."

Jace trudged after him. Delivering bad news to families was his least favourite part of the job. Unfortunately, whether he liked it or not, the Fillmores had a right to know that their daughters might never be coming back home.

CHAPTER 8

Swamps and Science

It had been a long night, but it had been so worth it. Finally, he had them. He chuckled to himself as he plunked his tired body in the armchair and brought the bottle to his lips. As the last several hours replayed in his mind, he couldn't believe his good fortune. Shivering though the parade to get a glimpse of them, then trailing them in the dangerous snowstorm had been risky. But after they'd slipped from the road and landed in the ditch right in front of him, it was providence at its finest. Thankfully, the pretty little elves already knew him, or he doubted they'd have climbed into his Jeep. He chugged his beer, belched, then swiped at his mouth with the back of his hand. Of course, they didn't have much choice. He cackled aloud before sobering.

The fear in their eyes when he'd had to use his gun to convince them they were to leave all their belongings behind, including their cell phones, bothered him. Evangeline tried to convince him they didn't own phones. Yeah, right. He wasn't born yesterday. He knew how obsessed the younger generation were with this type of social communication. In fact, he owned one himself, although his was a dumb phone. Pulling the gun on them was a last resort. He really didn't mean to scare them, but he needed them to produce those phones to prove that they hadn't already concealed them on their persons. On impulse, he'd had them hurl the devices into the snowy field. He knew the GPS trackers inside could be traced, but by the time they located the phones, the women would be long gone.

Thunderous banging on the door down the hall started up again. It was probably the feisty one. Evangeline didn't like being locked in the room and was very demonstrative with her objections. He sighed. That one was so much like … no, he wouldn't go there. Thinking of her sent him into a tailspin of depression for days.

That constant racket gave him a headache. He had to deal with it. Taking another large gulp of his beverage, he set the bottle on the floor beside him and stormed down the hallway. When he unlocked the door, a hurricane of fury charged at him. "Whoa, calm down there." He grabbed Evangeline's wrists to stop her from flailing at him. He'd been able to tell the twins apart because Evangeline had a brown café au lait birthmark on her chin. Like the one *she'd* had. Must be the reason she loved her coffee. Ha. Ha. He really was a funny guy. Why couldn't anyone else see that?

"Let us go, Percy! What do you want with us? I'm sure our parents and the police are out searching for us as we speak. You can't keep us here, wherever here is. They'll find us and you'll be in a heap of trouble."

He coaxed the feisty one inside the room and gently directed her toward the large queen mattress on the floor. When her heels hit it, she tripped, landing on her bottom. Her sister cowered in the corner, shaking like a leaf. The man pointed at Gabby. "Why can't you be more like your sister and accept your fate?"

"I have news for you. She hasn't accepted anything. She's afraid." Evangeline eyed the open doorway. Percy backed up until he blocked the exit in case she tried to make a run for it. Not that she'd get very far. Even if she managed to get outside, the snow was incredibly deep in the swamp. And they were far from civilization.

Evangeline shot to her feet again and parked her hands on her hips. "Where are we anyway? It feels like a nature museum or something with all those animal photos on the wall in the hallway. It's freezing in here and we're still in our elf costumes."

"Aw, quit your belly-aching. At least I let you keep your boots and coat, even if those flimsy green jackets won't keep you very warm. But you'll survive. I'd suggest you get some shut-eye—it's been a long night. And in case you're thinking of escaping, we're in a remote location, nowhere near home."

"How remote?" The whimpered question came from the corner. "I know we drove for hours in that horrible snowstorm."

A twisted grin broke across his face and he cackled hysterically. "That's for me to know and you to … not know." He laughed and slapped his knee. "I crack myself up." Little did the twins know that they were only about a half hour from their home. Playing mind games might keep them from trying to leave. Truth be told, he'd gotten terribly lost in that snowsquall. It wasn't until it let up a little that he realized he'd taken a wrong turn and missed the road to his place. He'd driven in circles for hours all because of that darn squall. Still, he couldn't complain. The nasty weather had provided the opportunity to finally fulfill his mission.

His home *was* kind of like a science museum. In fact, it was a visitor centre in a conservation area. He'd found it by accident a month ago while hunting in the swamp. And an even greater advantage was a service road leading to the place. Of course, it wasn't maintained this time of year, which made for tough going with that deep snow. Thankfully, Betsy, his aging Jeep Wagoneer was up to the task. Although the building was locked during the winter, he managed to break in a few weeks ago. An even bigger bonus was free heat, although it was kept at a minimal temperature so the pipes wouldn't freeze. But hey, far be it from him to complain. Since he was homeless, he was desperate for a warm place to stay for the winter. It had a small library with a few comfy chairs and couch where he slept, a washroom, lunchroom area with a kitchen, a smaller storage room with supplies, and a larger conference room. That was the girls' room. He'd purchased a cheap queen-sized mattress for them in anticipation of their stay.

Luckily, he'd been hired at the local coffee shop in Lighthouse Landing a few days after he'd found this place. The job didn't pay well, but it put food in his stomach and gas in Betsy. Hopefully, no one would come by to check on this building or he'd be in trouble. That's why he never turned the lights on.

"What do you want with us?" Evangeline whined. "I warned my sister about you, that you gave me the creeps whenever we visited the coffee shop."

He pressed a hand to his heart. "I'm terribly offended, although that's not the first time I've been told that. But if you only knew the truth, there would be no need to be afraid of me." He glanced at Gabby. "I have no plans to hurt either of you. I've been searching for you both for a long time. Now, get a few hours sleep and I'll make you something to eat when you get up."

"We want to go home," Gabby cried.

"Don't worry, my pets, or should I say elves; you'll learn to love it here." He hooted at his witty remark. This is your new home …" he paused and quirked an eyebrow, "at least until the spring. Before long, you'll learn to love me." His voice broke as he spun around, closed the door, and locked it securely. He swiped at his nose with the back of his hand. Getting all sentimental was for lily-livered fools. Taking a deep breath, he headed for his chair to finish off his beer. Time to celebrate. He finally had what he'd been looking for most of his life.

CHAPTER 9

Shattered Dreams in Duplicate

Kensington steered the squad car down the long snowy lane leading to the Fillmore Chicken Farm. Jace dreaded the awkward situation in front of them. *At least I'm only assisting in this case.* Kensington would assume the burden of being the bearer of upsetting news.

A chocolate lab bounded toward them, barking furiously at their car. Kensington made no attempt to exit the vehicle. Jace didn't blame him. Dogs were known to be protective creatures, and he knew from experience they often didn't like uniforms. Ed Fillmore opened the front door of the two-storey farmhouse, stepped to the edge of his porch, and whistled. The canine turned tail and raced to his owner.

When Mr. Fillmore put the dog inside, Kensington shut off the engine and stepped from the police cruiser. "Let's get this over with. I hate this part of my job."

"I hear you." Jace trailed the sergeant through the ploughed lane by a few steps. By the time they reached the front porch, Brenda stood at her husband's side in the doorway. Kensington and Kelly climbed the wooden steps leading to an attractive wrap-around covered porch.

"Please tell me you have good news." Brenda twisted her hands together.

"May we come inside?" Kensington removed his toque and gloves. The Fillmores stepped aside and allowed the officers entrance. All four stood on a large mat in the foyer.

Jace scanned his surroundings. The first thing that caught his eye was a flowering pink cactus cascading over the sides of a Duncan Phyfe table. His mother used to own a piece of furniture like that, along with a cactus with deep fuchsia blooms. For a split second he grew melancholy for the happy early childhood home he grew up in—until his father ruined it all. An ache skirted through him until he remembered. God was setting him free from the pain that he'd harboured for so long. He'd forgiven his father and was working at restoring the relationship—one that had not only been estranged for a number of years, but had made Jace a bitter and angry man. But that was the old Jace. Now Jace awakened each day with a goal to not look back at those crushing memories but ahead to hope-filled ones. Each day was a new beginning.

Jace continued to admire the Fillmore farm home. Gleaming hardwood floors led along a hallway to the kitchen. Immediately to his right was a burgundy carpeted staircase with rich oak handrails. To his left was a living area with a wood-burning fireplace and tan leather furniture, enclosed by glistening French doors. The overall appearance was pristine, homey, and pleasing to the eye. He could imagine he and Coral living here—could almost hear the pitter-patter of little feet overhead. As that thought barged in, his chest squeezed, and his angst rose. Would that dream ever be a reality?

Kensington's voice jolted him back to the present. "I'm sorry. I wish we had good news. We located your daughters' car in the ditch, about five minutes down the road from here. Sad to say, they weren't in it. The back driver-side door was left wide open and their purses remained inside. Officer Kelly conducted a thorough search for their cells but was unable to locate them even though the devices had been pinging a GPS signal from that location until this morning. The vehicle has now been taken to the station for a more thorough going over."

Brenda covered her mouth with a shaky hand.

"That's rather odd, isn't it? Maybe they tried to walk the rest of the way home, knowing they were close." Ed frowned.

"But why wouldn't they call us?" Brenda peered up at her husband as she clasped his upper arm tightly. "You could have driven down and picked them up and gotten their car out later."

Ed shrugged and covered his wife's hand.

"To be frank, we have some concerns. If the girls went for help, why wouldn't they take their purses or, at the very least, their mobile devices?" Kensington slapped his gloves against his hand as he spoke.

Ed shook his head. "Agreed. Something's not right. They never went anywhere without their phones. The obsession usually drove me crazy, but in a case like this it would have been invaluable to be able to call for help. It puzzles me that they didn't take them."

Jace nodded. "I'm with you. It doesn't make any sense."

"I just want my girls back." Brenda sniffled as moisture clouded her eyes.

"Have hope, sweetie. We have a fine police force that is working hard to find Gabby and Evangeline." He stroked her hair. "It'll all work out. You'll see."

Jace shoved his hands into his coat pocket. He marvelled at the strength the man exuded despite the worry he must also be experiencing. Would he be that strong in a time such as this? The Fillmores appeared to be a loving, devoted couple. Was that something he would have one day?

Kensington cleared his throat. "We'll get aerial surveillance covering the fields on either side of Concession 7 in case the girls decided to walk and, in their panic, left their personal belongings behind in their car."

Ed nodded.

"Like I mentioned, we've impounded their car. It'll also be dusted for prints. And we'll make sure this gets on the news pronto, so the public can be aware and alert for any signs of the twins."

The couple remained silent. Really, what could they say?

"Do you think someone abducted our girls?" Ed's trembling words caused his wife to sway beside him. Ed reached out and steadied her. "I'm sorry to bring this up, honey, but we can't bury our heads in the sand and pretend it's not a possibility."

"This may be a long shot, but had either of the girls been dating anyone recently whom you may have had concerns about?" Jace reached into a pocket and retrieved a pen and pad of paper. He still preferred the old method of taking notes.

From his peripheral vision Kensington glanced his way and quirked an eyebrow. What was that for? Was the sergeant surprised at Jace's outdated method of notetaking or the question itself?

"Neither girl was dating anyone. They have a core group of friends they hang around with, mostly from our church college and career group. But no boyfriends." Ed clung tightly to his distraught wife.

"Anyone in their workplace bothering them?"

Ed snorted. "Hope not. They work for us."

Brenda straightened and stared at her husband. "What about the migrant workers from Guatemala?"

"Nah!" Ed waved a hand through the air. "None of them have given me or the girls any grief that I'm aware of. They've been employed with us for several years. They're like family."

"All the same, perhaps we can have a talk with them." Jace looked up from his notepad. "When would be a good time for that? And I'll need names and addresses."

"They all share the old two-storey at the back of the property. You may catch some of them home now, but they often go into town on Saturdays to shop. Actually, they're all flying to Guatemala next Friday for the rest of December to spend time with their families over Christmas." Ed rattled off the names, pausing to help Jace spell most of them.

"We'll keep you updated the moment we learn anything new. And please do the same." Kensington reached for the doorknob as Jace tucked his notepad in his jacket pocket.

"We will. And please find our daughters," Ed pleaded as Jace followed Kensington onto the covered porch.

Kensington twisted his toque in his hands, then settled it over his silver locks. "I can assure you we're doing everything in our power to find them. Don't give up hope. There may be a logical explanation for what happened, and this could all be resolved happily and quickly."

Jace slipped his police-issue gloves on his hands and trudged through the deep snow beside his sergeant. Although he loved the positive spin that the sergeant left the distraught couple with, his mind was troubled. Would they find these girls alive?

Where in the world could they possibly be? The longer they were gone, the higher the chance of a horrible and tragic outcome.

CHAPTER 10

A Heart Exam

Coral's hot breath puffed in front of her face as she dug furiously at the massive snow-pile, hoping she could work off her frustrations as well as clear the front of her café. It was bitterly cold. How would she ever handle winters in this lakeside community? Tingling and pricking jabbed her fingers and toes. She couldn't handle being outdoors much longer. Her back ached—especially in that tailbone area—her arms and, worse yet, her heart ached. Hours of digging after she'd borrowed a shovel from her neighbour had only managed to clear snow in a small section of the parking lot and had done nothing to set aside her worries.

Thankfully, she hadn't had any customers after Luke. Most of the town was likely digging out from under the huge snowfall themselves. Which was fine since she wasn't up to seeing anyone.

A heaviness washed over her as scenes of this morning's painful encounter came to mind. How had she managed to hurt both men at the same time? Poor Luke had been an unintended victim—she'd had no reason to take her anger out on him. After all, he'd only come in to purchase treats for the police briefing. Instead, he'd been subjected to a screaming lunatic who'd ordered him to leave the premises. How horrible she felt when he'd followed her to the kitchen, opened the door, and politely asked to purchase baking for a meeting before he left. Even so, she'd been too upset to apologize while she loaded the pastry box with his choices. How much had he heard of the conversation between her and Jace?

Coral dropped her shovel, placed both hands on the small of her back, and stretched. A wave of dizziness gripped her, and she swayed. She latched onto the door handle of the shop until the police station across the street was on level ground. She sighed. Would she ever feel well again? Who knew a concussion could wreak such havoc for so long?

Waves of nausea churned in her stomach. Was that from dizziness or guilt? Probably more the latter. What had made her accuse Jace of stealing the job she'd wanted? Yes, she'd wanted it and it frustrated her that she couldn't apply. That much was true. But her health since she'd suffered injuries during her abduction a few months ago had made joining the force impossible. And Jace explained that he'd only considered the position after Kensington had contacted him to let him know Coral wasn't applying. Jace's motive was admirable—to be near her. Oh my! Gloved hands gripped the sides of her face. Why had she reacted the way she did, especially after such a precious gift from him the night before? And this morning's kiss? Despite the bitter cold, her cheeks warmed at the memory.

What had she gone and done? Had she pushed him away for good? Was it too late to fix things? Fatigue crashed over her. She peered into her café at the clock on the wall behind her counter. Two o'clock. No wonder her energy tank felt empty. She hadn't eaten since—wait a minute, last night's supper. She'd been too nervous to eat breakfast this morning, knowing Jace was coming.

Coral lifted the shovel and set it against an edge of the snow-pile before heading inside. Locking the door, she flipped the sign to *closed*. She really didn't expect any customers today and that was a good thing for a couple of reasons. Luke had cleared her out of about half of her baking and she'd burned a tray of cookies. Most importantly, she wasn't up to seeing anyone.

The muscles in her legs screamed for mercy as she climbed the stairs to her living quarters. After heating a bowl of potato-ham soup, she plunked in front of the television and hit the remote. Despite scrolling mindlessly through hundreds of channels, nothing caught her interest.

Coral finished her soup and set the bowl on the coffee table. She reached for a throw and wrapped herself in it, chilled from hours in that blustery weather. Exhaustion fell over her as if she'd been heavily drugged. And she didn't even fight it.

A rumbling sound awakened her. What time was it? Coral sat up and reached for her phone. A little before five o'clock. She'd slept for almost three hours. Yawning, she wandered to the window, slid a curtain panel aside, and stared out into the evening twilight. She couldn't believe it was almost dark already. Winters were not her favourite time of year—she was definitely more of a summer person.

Coral swallowed against a thickening in her throat that threatened to erupt into a sob. The ever-so-thoughtful Luke was clearing her parking lot and driveway with his snow blower—even after the way she'd treated him. An anvil of guilt sat on her chest. She cared about this man. How could she have treated him so rudely this morning? She let the curtain fall into place and made a bee-line to the couch, flopping hopelessly onto it. Quiet tears fell freely as she hugged the pillow against her chest.

Other than his belligerence when he was dealing with his father's impending death from liver cancer, Luke Degroot had been kindness personified since she'd known him. That difficult time in his life had coincided with Detective Jace Kelly's arrival in town to help apprehend the Lighthouse Landing Lament killer. But Luke had apologized for the way he'd acted, and she hadn't seen any signs of that type of behaviour since.

As Jace's shocked and hurt face appeared in her mind, she whimpered all the more. She sat up swiping at tears and reached for a tissue to blow her nose. What had made her react so harshly to Jace's announcement that he was the new sergeant for the Lighthouse Landing Detachment? Why couldn't she be happy for him? Instead, she'd been resentful and bitter. After all, she hadn't applied, and someone had to fill the position. To be totally honest, Jace was far more qualified than she was with his years as an OPP Homicide Detective in the big TO. Could she even have handled the pressure?

Truth be told, she'd been flabbergasted when Kensington suggested she apply. Perhaps he thought she came with more experience than she did. She should have been up front with

Kensington from the beginning and told him she wasn't qualified. Had she let the solving of her first case last year, The Bacon Murder, puff her up? Make her think she could handle anything? Although she'd played a role in apprehending Jeff Bacon for the murder of his wife, it was Jace's wisdom and job smarts that ultimately solved the case. A light flashed on in Coral's brain.

Pride and envy.

Jace had gotten the job she wanted. How incredibly selfish of her to not be happy for him. The man had made a huge sacrifice in leaving his long-standing job in Toronto in order to take a police sergeant's position in a small tourist town—all to be near her. He'd given her such a precious gift in more ways than one—dressing up like Santa in the bitter cold, not to mention the significance of the snow globe.

A verse trickled through her thoughts, something like, *God opposes the proud but gives grace to the humble*. Oh boy. Coral rested her head against the back of the couch and closed her eyes. *Dear God, I've suddenly seen myself for the prideful woman I am. Forgive me for thinking that I'm better than I am. I should have been happy for Jace, not lashed out at him in jealousy. I really don't even understand why I acted the way I did. Help me to think of others first, and please give me the strength to say I'm sorry. That doesn't come easy for me either. Pride again. I've been a very selfish person. For that, I'm also sorry. And please, God, I'm confused. I've come to love both men. Is that possible? Please guide me to the one you want me to spend the rest of my life with. If either of them. Perhaps I should stay single. But first things first, God. I need to find them both and apologize.*

CHAPTER 11

Emotions

A breaking news bulletin trailed across the bottom of the TV screen before local reporter Scott Forester appeared, microphone in hand, standing on the side of a snowy country road, his scarf flapping in the wind. Coral turned up the volume and listened intently.

"I'm on the scene of a mysterious incident. Evangeline and Gabby Fillmore, 22-year-old twins from the area have been missing since around eleven last night when they last checked in with their parents. They were driving home from the Lighthouse Landing Police's Annual Christmas Party. The women appear to have slid off the road in bad weather and possibly left their car in search of help. The 2012 Toyota Corolla was pulled from the ditch behind me a few hours ago." The cameraman zoomed in on tire tracks and disturbed snow in a deep gully along the side of the road.

"Police are asking for the public's help in locating the sisters. Anyone in the area of Concession Road 7 please check your property for signs of the women. Gabby and Evangeline are identical twins around five feet tall with shoulder-length blonde hair, blue eyes, and were last seen dressed in green elf costumes. Please notify the police immediately if you have any information regarding their whereabouts. Scott Forester, Shoreline News, signing off."

Dread hung over Coral. Something didn't feel right about this. Why would the women leave their car in a blinding snowstorm? Police always urged motorists to stay with their vehicle in cases like this. Coral hoped the worry she was experiencing for the girls was due more to her own emotional mood today and not something more sinister. Jace had told her this morning that the twins' cells were pinging a location along that road. If their phones were there, why weren't they?

Coral turned off the TV just as a loud knocking rattled her downstairs apartment door. Hopefully, it was Luke. She'd sent him a text telling him that they needed to talk. Coral's heart thumped erratically, and a sweat broke out on her brow. Maybe it was due to her warm kitchen, but she highly doubted it. Reaching behind her, she untied the strings and set her brown-and-pink-striped apron on the counter by the refrigerator. The dessert she'd removed from the oven a minute ago was cooling on top.

The knock came louder now. *Here goes.* Coral hurried down the steps, careful to hold the railing. She didn't need another tumble from a dizzy spell. At the thought of Luke's kiss that followed that crazy fall, a flustered feeling charged through her.

A gush of frigid winter air blew in with the tall officer. She took one look at his countenance and gulped. Who was more anxious—her or him? "Can you stay for a few minutes?" She shut the door against the blustery weather.

"Sure. I guess." He sniffed the air. "Is that cinnamon buns?"

"Yes." Coral smiled, her lower lip quivering with nerves as she watched him tug off his toque and gloves then hang his coat on the hook by the door. Next came his boots. "Follow me." Coral started up the steps.

"We're going upstairs?" Luke trailed behind her; his voice edged in curiosity.

"Yes." Coral wasn't surprised at his question. In all the time she'd known Luke, he'd only been to her apartment once—to retrieve a cushion for her the day she fell down the steps and hurt her tailbone.

"Have a seat." She pointed to the living room. "Are you hungry? I baked a pan of your favourite dessert."

"Actually, I'm famished. I worked late on the missing twins' case, then cleared your driveway and was about to head home for supper when I received your text." Luke scanned the room before seating himself on the far end of the couch. Placing his hands on his knees, he teetered on the edge of the cushion as if ready to bolt, one knee bouncing up and down. "What's this all about? You said you needed to talk to me."

Coral's eyes darted to Luke's then dropped to her feet. "I do. About this morning. I'm really, really sorry for the way I treated you." Her pulse accelerated and her palms grew clammy. She forced herself to make eye contact. "I was terribly upset with Jace, and unfortunately you became an unintended victim of my wrath. I didn't know you had even come in with the oven timer dinging and me fuming and …"

A nervous chuckle sliced the air.

Puzzled, she stared at Luke.

"Fuming? That's a word I haven't heard in a long time. But it's okay, Coral. I heard enough to understand what was going on. I was in the wrong place at the wrong time." He rose to his feet and opened his arms. "You've gotten upset for nothing. Come here."

So relieved Luke wasn't angry, she practically skipped across the room and fell into his arms, burrowing her face in his chest. "I'm sorry I hurt you," she blubbered, then tipped her head up to face him. "You are always so kind, even clearing out my driveway after the way I treated you. I don't deserve you."

Luke swallowed and his voice grew husky. "No, I don't deserve you."

Coral laughed softly. "Whatever do you mean? You're the one who's always doing kind things for me. What have I done for you?"

Luke sniffed the air. "Besides baking me my favourite dessert that I'm addicted to? Bringing me coffee the way I like it the minute I enter your café each day?"

Coral's lips turned up. "That hardly compares."

His gaze grew serious. "You were there for me when my father died, even after my behaviour hadn't been the best toward you and Jace. You forgave me, which meant the world to me."

Coral reached up and touched the side of his face. "How are you doing? It hasn't been that long since you lost him."

Luke placed a hand over hers. "See what I mean? You're doing it again." His eyes glossed over. "You care deeply. To be honest, it's tough some days. Mostly, I'm okay. It rips me apart to see my mother struggling with grief, though. I guess when you have truly loved someone for that long, it's like losing a part of yourself."

Coral's heart swelled, touched by Luke's concern for his mother and his insight into marriage. He seemed to know more than she did, as her father had abandoned the family early. Coral had no idea what true marital love looked like. Only what she'd read in books. Emotions overtook her sensibilities and she lost herself in the man's kind soul. Caught up in the moment, she leaned in close to kiss him.

Luke touched a finger to her lips.

She backed up slightly. "Is something wrong?"

"Absolutely."

"What? I don't understand."

"You know how I feel about you. But as far as I know, I haven't won your heart yet, have I? With Jace in the picture permanently, things are going to get messy. You can't leave us both dangling like this, Coral. Accepting your kiss would only make me want you more."

Tears welled until Luke blurred in front of her. What was wrong with her today? She didn't peg herself as one of those overly-emotional women, but all she'd done was cry. She had to get a grip. "There's something else you need to know." She sniffed.

Luke's chest rose as if he was inhaling deeply. "Oh boy. Hit me. This day can't get much worse."

"Jace was Santa last night. The gift was from him."

"I figured as much. After seeing him here this morning, I kind of put two and two together." He stepped away, slipping from her embrace. "Please don't play with my heart, Coral. Make your decision one way or the other. I can't do this anymore."

Luke clomped down the stairs, leaving her glued to the spot in shock. He hadn't even stayed for a cinnamon bun.

CHAPTER 12

A Listening Ear

Jace flipped his notepad closed as he and Kensington drove home in the dark. It had been a long afternoon interviewing all the men. "It was really fortunate that all six workers were home. I guess it helped that most businesses are closed because of the snowstorm. The workers insist they all drove home together after the Christmas parade last evening and hadn't left the house since. What do you think?"

"I think their alibis are valid. That old clunker of a van they share between them wouldn't get very far in that kind of weather, and did you notice it was buried under mounds of snow? It hasn't moved all night. The Guatemalan worker theory of yours was worth checking out, but I believe it's a dead end." Kensington slid to a stop at the intersection to Highway 21. The weather throughout the day had warmed up, and with the bright sunshine earlier, snow had melted on the roads and then frozen again as darkness set in and the temperature dropped.

"Crazy weather, eh?" Jace remarked as he called up his weather app.

Kensington chuckled. "This time of year the weather is all over the place."

"Tomorrow is supposed to be eight degrees Celsius. That's insane. From minus 13 with a wind chill of minus 22 yesterday to such a mild temperature tomorrow?" Jace paused as he contemplated the situation with the missing women. "On the bright side, if the Fillmore twins are lost in the elements, warming temperatures could be life-saving."

Kensington made a left turn toward Lighthouse Landing. He shook his head. "If they were outside all night, lying in a snowy field, and I hate to even think this let alone say it, they'd have frozen to death. But on the off chance that they found some type of shelter, like someone's barn, they could be fine. If that was the case, though, why wouldn't we have heard from them by now? You'd think they'd have walked to the nearest farmhouse come daylight when the storm abated and called their parents to let them know they were okay."

"I agree. The longer we go without any word, the more likely the outcome will not be good. What's our next course of action?" Jace tapped the console with a free hand as they reached the town limits.

"First, we'll see if any prints other than the twins' have been discovered on or in their car. Second, we need to find out if their cells were in the car and, if so, if Miller has been able to obtain any information from them."

Jace followed the sergeant into his office. "Have a seat while I summon Miller." Kensington pointed to one of the chairs.

A few minutes later, Officer Andrea Miller appeared in the doorway. "Yes, Serg?"

"Any news on the cell phones?"

"No phones were located in the car."

"Really?" Kensington sat up suddenly in his chair, his eyes huge. "That's bizarre. It doesn't make sense that a signal came from that location until early this morning."

Miller nodded. "I agree."

"How did your visit with Marie Nesbit go? Newton behave himself?"

"It went as expected. Crotchety Ralph Simmons denied he'd backed over his own blue box until he spied Newton's stern glare. Funny how the intimidation factor, without Newton saying a word, shocked the old codger into a truthful confession." Andrea snickered and coaxed a curl behind her ear.

"So Newton didn't use force on the old guy?"

"Absolutely not, sir. Not even an unkind word."

Jace listened intently to the conversation between the two. He was impressed that Kensington was checking up on the loudmouthed ex-military officer. But he was stymied about the missing cell phones.

"By the way, where is Newton now?" Kensington tapped a pen on his desk.

"Throwing together results from the fingerprinting. He plans to get you that report shortly."

"Okay, thanks, Miller. You're dismissed. Go home. See you tomorrow."

"You don't have to tell me twice." She whirled and, on her way out, slid a twisted smile at Jace. "See you, Kelly."

"Miller." Jace nodded.

Newton's towering frame filled the empty doorway left by Miller's departure. "Sir? Do you have a minute?"

"Fingerprint report?" Kensington's eyebrows raised.

"Nothing discerned but the twins', sir." Newton held out the paper to his boss.

Jace couldn't help but note the width of the officer's biceps. A tattoo of some type of medieval sword ran the length of Newton's right forearm, adding to the man's intimidation factor.

"I heard your encounter with Mr. Simmons went well." Kensington studied the information on the report.

"It did." Newton frowned—his displeasure with the case still evident by the downcast turn of his lips and clenched fists.

"Fine, dismissed."

Newton trudged from the room, his heavy footfalls echoing in the hallway.

Kensington leaned back in his chair, his gaze zeroing in on Jace. A churning began in the pit of his stomach. What was that look about? "You seem a tad off, Kelly. Are you having second thoughts about assuming my position come January?"

Jace grimaced. Was he that easy to read? He blew out a breath. "Yes and no, sir. It's not the position that has me worried, it's other things."

Kensington's forehead wrinkled. "Female other things, by any chance?"

Jace fidgeted in his chair. Nothing escaped this wise man. He could only hope that, when he held the top position, insight would be his friend, too.

"Not good to keep things bottled up Kelly."

Was Kensington offering to let him unload? Perhaps lend a little advice? The sergeant seemed in no hurry to pack things up for the night. "Close it." Kensington waved a hand toward the wooden door with a glass window at the top.

Jace leaned forward, rested his elbows on his thighs, and locked his hands beneath his chin. Did he really want to burden his supervisor with personal stuff? It *would* be kind of nice to get another man's perspective, particularly that of a man he admired. Before he could change his mind, Jace shot to his feet and hurried toward the door. Hand on the knob, he debated whether to bolt instead. How childish and immature that would look. After closing the door, he took his seat again, his eyes flitting around the room aimlessly, everywhere but on his boss. "You don't know much about me, sergeant, and maybe that's a good thing or you wouldn't have hired me."

Kensington quirked an eyebrow but kept silent.

"Without going into too many details about my past, it was a troubled one. My father abandoned my mother and me when I was ten years old. My mother died not long after, and I never saw my dad again until a year ago." Jace took a deep breath, digging for strength. "I didn't realize the bitterness I'd held for my father all that time had not only turned into hatred, it was crippling me, on the job and off. My nickname on the force in TO was Catastrophe Kelly." Jace had been studying the picture of Kensington's family on the wall but forced himself to shift his gaze to his supervisor. When Kensington didn't even flinch, a little of the tightness left Jace's shoulders. He'd been worried that letting out that nasty bit of personal information might cause the sergeant to rescind his job offer. Either he'd already known, or it didn't matter.

"No one wanted to work with me; partners only lasted a day—until Officer Coral Prescott." Jace's grip was so tight on the arms of his chair that his palms grew sweaty. He let go and rubbed them on his pants. "At first I thought she would be as incompetent as the others, but there was something different about her. Despite my attempts to stay detached, within a week of being on the Bacon

Murder Case together, feelings developed between us. I thought it was all one-sided, but when she kissed me ..." Jace bit his bottom lip. "Anyway, she challenged me to get help for my bitterness and to seek out God—both impossible hurdles in my mind. After the arrest of Jeff Bacon last year, I was devasted when she walked out of my life and left the force. Devastated and confused. I spent several months in a deep, dark place." Jace raked a hand through his hair, chancing another look at Kensington.

The older man had rested his elbows on the chair, his fingers steepled in front of his mouth as he studied Jace intently. Jace's throat constricted. How did Kensington feel about God? Was he a man of faith? Would he object to what Jace was about to tell him? No matter, he'd gone this far, he may as well get the whole story out.

"Briefly, I made peace with my father and, even though progress is slow, I'm working at fully forgiving him. And I found God in a most unusual way. But that story, I'll leave for another day."

Jace leaned against his chair, his energy spent. Why was it that emotional topics zapped your energy almost as much as physical ones? Of course, he also hadn't slept much last night.

"I'm always happy to hear progress in a man's personal life. In case you're wondering, I'm a person of faith as well. So is my wife. I couldn't do this job and balance my marriage without God's strength on a daily basis. So, what is really troubling you?"

Jace rubbed the back of his neck as he contemplated his messed-up situation. Did he really want to share this next part? Of course, it might help to get another man's counsel. "You know how I readily jumped into your Santa role this year?"

Kensington chuckled. "I do. And I'm thankful. I really wasn't up to it. I've been fighting a cold, and sitting on a float in that weather wouldn't have been wise."

Jace got to his feet and paced the small office. "I guess I should back up a little." He shoved his hands in his pocket and stared down at his shoes. "A few months ago, while Coral was hospitalized due to injuries from Triple L's abduction, I decided to propose marriage. When I entered her hospital room, I ..." Jace's stomach swirled. He thought he'd gotten over the shock of that scene. "I caught Luke and Coral kissing."

"Ouch." Kensington groaned.

"When Luke turned to leave, he got in my face and challenged me, saying something to the effect that he loved Coral and was going to fight for her."

Kensington let out a low whistle. "Oh boy. That's tough. What did you do?"

Jace stopped pacing, whirled, and faced the man. "Something very foolish. After Luke left the room, I dropped the giftbag containing the ring and ran—after informing Coral that the ball was in her court. That she needed to decide between the two of us. Of course, she didn't know there was a ring in the bag at that point. I didn't hear from her after that, so I assumed her choice was Luke. But then ..."

Deep in thought, he hadn't realized how long he'd paused until Kensington rolled a hand through the air. "But then ... I was praying, had been praying, about the situation with Coral and felt God leading me to not only come to see her but to apply for your position. I also had a special gift made for her with personal significance."

Kensington smiled. "Is that why you singled her out at the party last night?"

Jace's heart leapt at the memory. "Yes." His cell buzzed in his pocket. He pulled it out, studied the screen, and froze. A text from Coral. How in the world did she do that? And she wanted to talk. Well, he didn't want to talk to her. Not right now. He shoved it into his pocket.

"How was the gift received?"

"Very well, I thought. We had a brief and wonderful reunion this morning until ..."

"Until?"

"When she learned I would fill your shoes in January, she became irate, accusing me of stealing the job she wanted."

"Hmm. That seems like an odd reaction, especially since she turned it down because of her health."

Jace clenched his jaw, memories of the encounter still tender in his mind. "I agree. She was livid and ordered me out of her café, even after I explained that I did it for our relationship." Kensington rubbed his chin, as he often did while thinking. "I believe there's something else going on here. And it may have to do with Luke DeGroot. They've grown close over the last few months and have been seen together around town a few times. Some think they're a couple. Sorry to saddle you with that news, but I thought you should know."

Beads of sweat broke out on Jace's brow. Although it wasn't really news to him, he'd figured as much. Perhaps he was too late. Had he handled things all wrong with Coral? Dropping the ring and running was cowardly, he saw that now.

He turned when a warm hand landed on his shoulder. Kensington stood at his side. "This is definitely a matter for more prayer. If you felt God calling you here to Lighthouse Landing, then trust that. Keep waiting for His leading. I cannot direct you on the other matter as Luke DeGroot is also a fine, upstanding man and I don't want to interfere. In my opinion, Coral would win with either of you. You need to seek God's direction in this. But I'd encourage you to be honest and tell her how you feel."

Jace's chest felt as if a crushing weight sat on it. "Thank you for listening. It's been a long day and we have two women to find. I'm sorry for taking up your time. See you tomorrow." A little embarrassed at pouring out his heart, Jace strode to the door, flung it open, and promptly ran smack into Miller. "Oops! Terribly sorry." Jace grabbed her shoulders to steady her, then quickly let go.

"No worries. Totally my fault. I was in a rush to give the serg a message before I left." Her hands rested against his chest, typing a sizzling invitation through her fingers. How brazen of her to squeeze his pecs in front of the sergeant. Judging from the fact that Jace's back was to his boss, Kensington probably didn't witness the inappropriate sexual advance though.

Jace's eyes widened at her boldness as he removed her hands. His emotions ran at a feverish pitch, but they had nothing to do with Miller. He took a step backward into the sergeant's office. Why was it that the women who were attracted to him didn't interest him in the least, but the one who had captured his heart seemed elusive? He'd definitely need to deal with this officer's behaviour once he was in command.

Miller stood in the doorway, blocking his escape. "Boss, that pesky news reporter is on the phone for you. He wants to know if there are any more updates on the Fillmore case."

Kensington sighed. "I'll take it, thanks."

Miller finally turned and left, her tiny hips whipping from side to side as she made her way down the hallway. Kelly looked away. Good grief. That woman was a bundle of raging hormones, and they seemed to be aimed in his direction.

While Kensington conversed with the reporter, Jace's cell vibrated and he reached for it. Another message from Coral. She desperately needed to talk to him, apparently, but Jace was in no mood. He was still angry from this morning's confrontation, especially after all he'd done to try and show her how he felt. Nope. He'd let her stew a few days, or possibly a little longer. Maybe forever.

Kensington grumbled as he slammed the phoned down. "That reporter can be irritating at times, although he's good at his job. His reporting has played to our advantage on numerous occasions and helped us solve cases, but we do need to make sure we don't give him too much information." The sergeant rose, stalked toward Jace, and flipped the light switch. The room went dark. "Go home, Kelly, and get a good night's sleep. I'll keep you informed if anything breaks on the Fillmore case during the night."

"You don't have to twist my arm. Goodnight, Serg." Exhausted, Jace trudged down the hallway. Would Coral and he ever be able to figure things out? He sighed as he slipped into his boots, toque, and parka. A worrisome thought flitted through his mind. If Coral chose DeGroot, how in the world would he ever work in this community? He'd hate to mess up Kensington's

retirement plans at such short notice, but it would be torture to stay here in Lighthouse Landing and watch the two of them together.
    Absolute torture.

CHAPTER 13

Melting Snow and Broken Hearts

Coral could only listen to the hymns, as every time she opened her mouth to join in her lower lip quivered and her throat tightened. Every song brought her emotions to the surface all over again. Pressing her lips together, she allowed the music to flood her soul and the words to sink into her heart. When the pastor began his sermon, the verse he shared hit her hard. She couldn't remember it word for word or even the Scripture reference, but it impacted her all the same—that God required his people to act justly, love mercy and walk humbly with Him.

There was that *humble* word again. When God convicted a person of something, there was no denying it. The painful scene with Jace—when she'd accused him of stealing the job she wanted—played out in her mind again and she squirmed in her seat. *I get it, God. I truly do. Instead of being happy for Jace, I was jealous and prideful, not humble in the least. I'm sorry for my actions and I'm trying to seek forgiveness from him, but he won't return my messages.*

Suddenly, it seemed as if God directed her to the man seated on the far side of the congregation across from her. Her pulse sped up at the sight of Jace Kelly, and she shook her head in sheer amazement. Had God arranged this? He'd not only convicted her of her pride yesterday, he'd confirmed it with a verse today and then brought the man to her so she could apologize.

The rest of the service flew by in a blur. Every couple of minutes, Coral shot another look at the detective. Did he know she was here? Their eyes hadn't connected. Although his outward appearance was flawless, his face betrayed an inner turmoil … one that she'd probably caused. The moment the service was over, she'd corner him and attempt to make things right between them.

At the last words of the closing hymn, Coral's gaze flicked to the row again, where Jace had been seated. Disappointment flooded through her at the empty spot on the pew. No! He couldn't have left already. Coral grabbed her purse, coat, and Bible, and fled down the aisle before she could get caught behind a slow-moving, chatty crowd of parishioners.

Her speed didn't help. She scanned the church grounds and parking lot but detected no sign of him. What type of vehicle did Jace drive? He'd walked to her café yesterday due to the deep snow. And she'd only ever seen him drive a black SUV belonging to the OPP.

Coral was determined to find the man. She slipped into the driver's seat of her car and texted him again. She waited. And waited. Silence. Now she was angry. She bit her lip hard. How in the world could she apologize if he wouldn't answer her texts? Exasperated, Coral grabbed the steering wheel and let her head flop against her arms. *Please God, help me figure this out. Create an opportunity for me to talk to Jace and set things straight. I know he's angry, but this is pure torment. I need this resolved, one way or another.*

Coral jumped at the knock on her driver's side window. Looking up, she squinted at the shape in front of her, darkened by the blinding sun behind him. Jace Kelly? She lowered her window and was immediately enticed by the familiar smell of his cologne, carried in on a gust of wind. "Yes?" She squeaked.

"Are you okay? The parking lot is empty. I thought maybe you'd passed out at the wheel. Thankfully, you weren't driving."

Maybe he cared after all? She scanned the church lot. The only vehicle present, other than hers was a shiny, newer model Chevy Silverado. So that's what he was driving. How long had she been collapsed against her steering wheel? Had she fallen asleep while pouring her heart out to God? Succumb to another dizzy spell? "I've been trying to get in touch with you. Why haven't you answered my messages?"

"I'm here now." His eyes grew hooded, brooding almost, marring his powerful good looks if that was even possible. He was minus a warm coat and wearing a dark grey suit with an aqua shirt. The tie with diamonds of peach on a bluish-green background not only complemented the outfit, it accentuated his features. Jace Kelly was such a handsome man that a quiver travelled through her body. Could be from the nippy breeze sailing in the window. "Do you have a minute to talk? I thought maybe we could go for a walk. I need to get something off my chest also."

He wants to talk?

"A walk? It's freezing and with all that snow?" In spite of her words, Coral's heart quickened at the invitation. What made her complain about the weather? Must be nerves. She'd climb Mount Everest in a blizzard for a chance to apologize to the man. What did he want to say to her? He didn't look happy. At all.

"The sun is warm. In fact, my weather app says it's ten degrees. I'm shocked at how much snow has already melted from yesterday's storm. You won't freeze for a few minutes. This won't take long."

Oh no. That sounded ominous. Was he ending things between them? Coral slipped from the car and treaded slowly behind Jace, who was strolling toward the lake. The parking lot had been mostly cleared, yet puddles from melted snow covered icy sections. Even so, as she forced one foot in front of the other, her tenuous crawl was more from nerves than the slippery conditions.

"This view is phenomenal, isn't it?" Jace remarked as she reached his side and followed his gaze. The little Baptist church was perched on a bluff overlooking Lake Huron, and she had to admit that the scene, despite the wild wind, was spectacular.

Was this a stall tactic? Could she blame him? She guessed that neither of them wanted to deal with the elephant in the room. "It sure is. I didn't realize the church had erected stairs to the beach." Coral would have marvelled at everything her eyes took in if it weren't for the unrest inside her. The brisk wind made her wish she'd secured her hair in a ponytail as it flew around her face. White caps far out on the lake created the illusion of tips of vanilla frosting on a cake. Was she hungry? Or did she spend too much time in the kitchen? She couldn't escape the irony—the turbulent water mirrored the tumult in her heart.

"I'm sorry." They both spoke in unison.

Coral turned and their eyes connected. "What? Why are you sorry? I'm the one who needs to apologize. I have no idea what you want to say, but can I please go first?"

Jace's hands had been squeezing the wooden railing at the top of the stairs. He shoved them in his pockets. "Fine."

"I … um … I …" Coral felt as though she might lose her breakfast. Nausea swirled inside her and her mouth went completely dry. Why was it so hard to get the words out? Wetting her lips, she plunged forward. "I'm sorry for the way I acted yesterday morning. I shouldn't have gotten angry hearing about your new position. My reaction was prideful and completely inane, especially since I'd already turned the position down." Jace's eyes felt like lasers probing her conscience. "I guess it was frustration with my health bubbling over." Her apology came out in pauses and stutters.

"Your health?" He frowned. "Are you having a setback with Celiac disease?"

"No. Now it's lingering symptoms from the concussion."

"I'm sorry. I didn't realize." His eyes softened a little before he glanced away.

"God hates pride so much that he opposes the proud. I don't want God against me. Again, I'm really, really sorry. I'm truly happy for you, Jace, and I've no doubt that you'll make a fine police sergeant. To be honest, even if my health hadn't deterred me, I don't have enough experience to feel competent taking on that role. I let Kensington's job offer swell my head. Pride again. And to think you moved here for me—for us—only adds to my guilt." She studied a trail of melting snow dripping off the railing.

Jace was silent.

"Do you forgive me?" She reached for his hand and squeezed it tightly. "Because I don't know what I'll do if you don't."

Slowly he angled his neck toward her, his eyes studying their clasped hands. "Forgiven."

The heaviness in his voice and sadness in his eyes didn't alleviate her guilt much. It pained her that she had really hurt him.

An awkward quiet hung in the air until Coral managed a weak smile in his direction. "Thank you. Go ahead. What did you have to say?"

Jace tugged his hand out from under hers and shoved it in his pants' pocket. He shifted from one foot to the other. "I need to back up to your hospital stay. I was cowardly by running and not proposing. Actually, I hadn't planned to do it that way, but I was devastated when Luke kissed you. Then when he told me he was in love with you and would fight for you, I was thrown completely off kilter. In hindsight, I didn't handle things well." The corners of his mouth dipped downward.

Coral's chest constricted as she recalled that scene. She wished she could forget it.

He stared at his feet and rocked back and forth on his heels. "I'm sorry for the way I left things, but even before the kiss I had sensed an attraction between the two of you—that your heart was conflicted. That's why I left the ball in your court, so to speak. Was I wrong?"

A pang of guilt stabbed her in the chest, and she couldn't look him in the eye. She tipped her head to watch a seagull dip and soar on air currents as if it didn't have a care in the world. Oh, how she wished she could be that bird right now.

"Coral? I need an answer on this. Was I wrong? Am I wrong?" He rested his hands on her shoulders, his eyes imploring her to answer.

"Um ... yes and no." Coral wrung her hands together, partly from angst and partly for warmth. "If you had proposed that day, I would have said yes." Her eyes connected with his shocked ones.

Dropping his hands from her shoulders, he grabbed the handrail, as if to steady himself. "Wow! Are you giving it to me straight?"

"I'm being totally honest with you. I was as shocked as you when Luke kissed me. Hadn't seen it coming. I didn't know how to react because the man was losing his father. In fact, he died in ICU that very day. Luke is a really great guy, but it was only friendship at that point. But when you disappeared for so long, I was heartbroken and hurt and … Luke and I became close. I couldn't understand why you dropped the ring and ran. I figured that in a few days, after you got over the initial shock of that unexpected kiss from Luke, you would contact me. When it never happened, I thought you'd changed your mind."

Coral's voice broke. "Your silence really hurt. To be honest, I was confused. Why didn't you fight for me? I heard you tell Luke that you would do that. But you didn't. And Luke, well, he's been there for me. He *did* fight. More than that, he's been taking care of me. I'm still struggling with aftereffects from the concussion and experience dizzy spells and headaches. Some days I can't even open the café. Luke always checks up on me, helps with deliveries, and clears the snow from my driveway and parking lot. At the least, he's become a very good friend. At the most … I don't know."

Jace took a deep breath and appeared to be holding it. He slowly exhaled and raked a hand through his hair. "I'm sorry about the silence. Although it appears that I wasn't fighting for you, I was waiting for God's direction. I prayed continually through these last few months. One day as I stared out my high-rise window, I felt God's prompting to apply for Kensington's position. At least I thought I did. After your reaction yesterday, I questioned whether I heard God or if it was my own desires getting in the way." Jace clutched her hands. "I've missed you so much, Coral. When we kissed yesterday, it was perfect, completing, and filled me with such joy that I almost came undone. If you don't feel the same, then what are we doing? I can't stay near you if you decide on Luke. It will be too painful. I need an answer, because if you choose Luke, Kensington will have to find another replacement. So what is it?"

Pressure built up in Coral's chest and she exploded, yanking her hands from his and pummelling his chest with her fists. "Why didn't you fight for me? My heart was broken, and I was terribly confused. I loved you, Jace Kelly. Now … I don't know." Her cries cut the air as tears threated again. Some spilled over and trickled down her cheeks. She was sick of crying but was helpless to stop the flood. Releasing all those weeks of pain was cathartic.

Jace reached for her clenched fists, clasped them, and pulled her against him. Did she hear him groan? He rested his head against hers and wrapped his arms around her tightly. Her tears slowed and eventually stopped as he held her close. She didn't know how long she remained in his embrace, but it was a healing place that she never wanted to leave.

They both turned in the direction of the building at the sound of a squeaking hinge. The church custodian had a green garbage bag in his hand and was heading toward a dumpster at the back of the church. He glanced at them briefly, did a quick wave with a free hand, and tromped through the snow toward the metal bin.

Coral shivered, and Jace reached for her hand. "You're cold. Let's go."

They were silent as they walked hand in hand toward Coral's car. When they stopped at her driver's door, Jace freed a lock of her hair that had stuck itself to her wet cheek, then cradled her face in his hands. "I love you, Coral. It's not my feelings that are in question here. It's yours. Analyze your heart and do it fast. Or I'm gone."

CHAPTER 14

Percolating Nerves

Percy placed his burner phone on the bookshelf beside him as a smile came over his face. It had been brilliant of him to purchase one—no chance of tracing anything to him. Yep, he was smarter than the average bear. But truth be told, he hadn't thought a few things out. Snatching the women unexpectedly in the middle of the storm had been a huge opportunity but left him unprepared. Why hadn't he thought about clothing and food ahead of time in case his plans came to fruition sooner than expected? It was comical to see Evangeline and Gabby in those green elf costumes. He had to admit they were cute as buttons. Still, they couldn't stay in them forever. Oh well. There were worse things in life—like being deprived of love for so long—the reason he'd needed to see that cockamamie shrink in the first place.

A tsunami of irrationality barrelled over him and his heart beat erratically. Percy jumped to his feet and paced the room, smacking his forehead with the palm of his hand. No wonder he felt like he was about to come unglued. He'd forgotten to renew his prescription for anxiety meds, and he'd swallowed the last pill a few days ago. He'd have to leave the girls and drive to the pharmacy in town. That wasn't a huge problem. No one could link him to the twins' disappearance, which he imagined was all over the news by now. The only thing that worried him was running into one of his coworkers since he'd called in sick for his Saturday and Sunday shifts. After all, Lighthouse Landing wasn't a very big town. He checked the time on his watch. Four o'clock. Hopefully, the pharmacy would stay open until five or six on a Sunday afternoon.

Percy grabbed the sides of his head as he treaded the cream-coloured carpeting in the library. *What to do. What to do. What to do.* Beads of sweat dotted his brow. *Calm down, Perk.* He chuckled at the nickname he'd tried to concoct for himself at work.

All his life, he'd been made fun of for his unusual name, so at the beginning of his training at the coffee shop, he insisted he be called Perk instead of Percy—fitting since he percolated coffee all day. He guffawed loudly, slapping at his thighs. He really was a brilliantly funny guy, coming up with such an ingenuous name. Too bad it didn't stick. In fact, someone starting calling him Percy Sprinkles, like the brightly-coloured candy decorations on iced donuts. Grr. Given the chance, he'd like to decorate that sassy co-worker's head with a pot of hot coffee followed by whipped cream and sprinkles.

Thinking of donuts, his stomach growled, reminding him that it was getting near supper time. Maybe he should pick up some fast food when in town since he was low on groceries. For breakfast this morning he'd offered the girls the muffins he'd brought home the night he'd abducted them, but they'd declined. Abducted was really a nasty word—how could you abduct something that was rightfully yours?

Should he even worry about food? He couldn't get either of them to eat anything anyway, only drink water. He shook his head. Eventually, they'd grow accustomed to their new surroundings. When they did, their appetites would return. He hated the fear he detected in their eyes whenever he opened the door to their room, but that couldn't be helped. Once they understood the honest truth, things would be very different. He'd tell them soon.

Another wave of angst zipped through his entire body and he yanked at his hair then stared at the clump of dark brown tresses tangled between his fingers. Why didn't he feel any pain? If he didn't stop taking his frustrations out on his scalp, he'd be bald before long.

Percy reached for the key to the girls' room that he kept hidden behind a *Birds of North America* book on the top library shelf. His hands trembled so violently he could barely get the key in the hole. Meds. He really needed his meds. He took a deep, calming breath—a trick the shrink had taught him. Usually it didn't work, but he had to try. He couldn't let the girls see him this way. The door creaked open and he paused. Where in the world could they be?

A dark shape came at his face so fast he was helpless to stop it. He heard the jingle and the crack at the same time he experienced a sickening pressure on his face. Screeching in pain, his hands instinctively flew to his nose. What had just happened? His eyes watered and his vision blurred. He could barely make out Evangeline standing there, green elf boot in hand, a look of satisfaction on her face. A warm sticky liquid poured over his mouth and down his chin as he cradled his injured nose. "Why you little demon. I think you broke my snout. The heel went right up my nostril."

A dastardly grin crossed Evangeline's face as she jingled the boot toward him and giggled aloud. "Snout? What are you, a pig?"

Percy lunged toward the audacious twin, but a sudden stabbing pain on the top of his foot stopped him and he howled in agony. Stumbling into the room, he collapsed onto his knees. He whirled to see Gabby crouching behind the door. She had rammed him hard with the sharp spikey heel of another one of those dratted boots. Who would have thought footwear could be used as weapons against him? If he'd only known ...

Both women flew past him. Evangeline gave him a shove on the way out, knocking him onto an elbow. "No way!" He clambered to his feet and hobbled to the door, managing to wedge his foot into the opening just in time. Which was good because he'd foolishly left the key in the lock. Imagine if they'd locked him inside.

The horror on Gabby's face tugged on his heartstrings as he reached out and grabbed her arm. "No way are you locking me in here, pumpkin." No sense being upset with this one. The whole breakout was probably planned by her foolhardy sister, who was nowhere to be found. How brave was that? To leave your timid-as-a-rabbit twin to fend off the bad guy. But hey, he wasn't a bad guy. It was about time the world got that straight.

Using as little force as possible, he pushed Gabby back into the room and locked the door. It broke his heart to hear her screaming and crying for her sister, despite the fact that the little sweetie had punctured his foot. Most likely Gabby had been cajoled into being her twin's accomplice in crime. Percy limped along the hallway, feeling worse than the time he'd gotten into that bar fight at Marv's with four burly motorcycle dudes.

Where was Evangeline? He spied her cowering in a corner of the kitchen by the sink, wielding a frying pan high over her head. "Stay back. I'm not afraid to use this."

Percy laughed, then choked on a mouthful of blood. He reached for the tea-towel and held it against his nose. "Put the pan down. It's meant for frying things, not nailing your father." His voice sounded weird, but then again it would with his nasal passages plugged with blood.

Evangeline's eyes widened, then narrowed suspiciously while she gritted her teeth. "My father? Ha. You're delusional. Ed Fillmore is my father. You're not even old enough. You need mental help, mister."

Percy limped toward her and held out a hand. "You are trying my patience. Give me the skillet or you won't get any eggs for breakfast."

"Oh, I'm scared. Like that's going make me hand it over." She swung it toward him. "Don't come any closer. I'm warning you."

"Do you think I'm worried? You may have ambushed me with that boot, but do you seriously think your skinny little elf-self stands a chance against me? You're wasting your energy." His eyes hardened.

She paused, worry scooting across her face, then lifted the pan high again. "I'll never stop trying to get away from you, you sick man. Have you considered your injuries? You're limping and your voice sounds like a honking Canada goose. Before long, you're going to regret abducting us."

"That's enough." Percy tossed the bloody towel into the sink and charged toward her. Before she could bring the pan down on his head, he grabbed her wrist and squeezed it so hard that the pan clanged to the floor. She fought his hold, kicking at him with a socked foot until he managed to grab a leg and had her hopping like a stork. "Are you quite done? I really don't want to hurt you. Please, get that through your head."

"I want to go home. Please let us go," Evangeline wailed.

"Right now, you're going back into your room with your sister, who is sobbing her heart out." He dragged her through the hallway, reached into his pocket for the key, unlocked the door, and shoved her inside. Gabby ran toward Evangeline and they fell into each other's arms. "I'm heading into town for a few hours to get supplies. I'll feed you when I get back."

He slammed the door, limped to the bathroom, and stared in the mirror. He gasped at the bloodied monster staring back at him. His left eye had the beginnings of a purple ring around it, and was his nose tipped to one side? That was probably the crack he'd heard while being nailed with the jingling boot. He'd need ice for that nose, which would hopefully keep the swelling to a minimum. He'd hate to have to see a doctor to get his nose set. After all, how would he explain the injury? He could say that he ran into a tree while hunting in the dark. If it came down to it, he'd lie if he had too. Anything to cover the truth.

That brazen attack had marred his good looks. Still, it made him feel good that Evangeline thought he wasn't old enough to be her dad. He spat into the sink and washed away the blood from his face with a cloth. Hopefully his nose would stop bleeding soon.

Bending down, he removed his red-stained sock and stared at the puncture hole on the top of his foot. Drat! It was ugly and sore, but at least his foot wasn't broken, and he wouldn't need stitches.

It was hard slipping on his left boot and he winced as he forced his foot inside. Must be starting to swell already. He limped through the house, grabbed his truck keys, and hobbled outside through the snow. Seconds later, Betsy's engine roared to life.

He ground his teeth as he struggled through pain in various parts of his body. Those girls were more trouble than he'd anticipated. Hopefully, things would settle down soon. Perhaps, if he brought them their favourite treats, they would grow to accept their fate. He knew Evangeline liked those sour-cream-glazed donuts and Gabby the double-chocolate ones from their visits to the coffee shop. Yes, that's what he'd do.

But wait. Should he chance the drive-through at the coffee shop? Someone might recognize him or his vehicle. He shook his head and immediately regretted the impulsive move as a throbbing began in his nose. Visiting the drive-through was a bad idea, especially since he'd called in sick. He'd have to think of something else to bring home to appease them.

He mulled over his future without a job. Thankfully, he'd socked enough savings away to hide with the twins until the search died down. Then he'd move them to a new location where he'd have to seek employment. Although, he really didn't know where that new location was yet. He figured he had until spring to find it. That's when Conservation employees would most likely come by to reopen the visitor centre. As his vehicle jostled along the bumpy service road, every movement sent pain through his face. He gently touched his nose, trying to assess if it was broken or not. Darn that Evangeline. Who would have ever thought to use a boot as a weapon? Only his girl. Thankfully, a good dose of meds should help calm his anxieties and dull the pain. He may even treat himself to a second dose.

CHAPTER 15

Erratic Behaviour

"Give me that prescription now. I don't care if you have to call the Health Minister for approval. I need it." The fortyish-looking man grabbed at his hair.

Coral was next in line behind the agitated customer at the pharmacy counter. What was wrong with him? Was he in some sort of drug withdrawal? She reached in her purse and grabbed her phone, ready to call 911 if the situation warranted.

The young female pharmacist raised her palms. "Sir, calm down, or I'll have to call police. According to our records your refills have run out. You'll need to make an appointment to see your doctor."

The man shifted from one foot to the other. "I only moved here a few months ago. I don't have a local doctor and my psychiatrist is in Hamilton. Just call him. His name is Dr. Benjamin Barnes."

"I'm sorry, that's not possible. It's Sunday and he won't be in his office. This will have to wait until Monday morning. Can you please step away? There's a long line behind you."

"Can't you give me one pill until tomorrow? I'm in a bad way." The man's voice was pleading and desperate.

Coral's heart softened a little. Perhaps it was a true oversight and the guy desperately needed those meds. She understood from her time as a police psychologist that medication could be crucial for those suffering from mental health stress and anxiety.

The pharmacist shook her head. "I'm sorry."

"Ridiculous system." The man whirled and hobbled through the store, still muttering aloud. "Gotta get my alcohol then back to my girls. The beer store better be open or someone's gonna pay."

Someone's gonna pay? Coral's soft heart wasn't soft any longer—more like worried at the man's threat. After observing one half-open eye, a flattened, cockeyed-nose, and dried blood on his upper lip, she wondered if he'd been in a fight. Her police mind kicked into high gear. How old were his daughters? Was there a mother in the picture? Who was going to pay?

She moved out of line and discreetly followed the man to the front of the store. Peering through the pharmacy windows located behind the checkouts, she scanned the parking lot until she saw him climbing into an older-model, rusted, bronze Jeep. When he sailed past her window, she typed in the license plate number in the notes section on her phone, in case it might be needed. Once a police officer, the training didn't leave.

Coral wandered to the back of the store and took her place in line again. A few minutes later it was her turn. "Prescription for Coral Prescott, please."

Did the pharmacist's hands shake as she typed in the amount Coral owed?

Coral tapped her debit card on the machine. "Are you okay? I overheard everything with that combative customer a few minutes ago."

The pharmacist nodded. "I'm fine, but I was ready to call the police. He made me very nervous."

"I don't suppose you're allowed to say what med the guy was in desperate need of? Maybe even the guy's name?" Coral figured the answer would be no, but she had to try.

"Sorry, patient confidentiality." The woman stapled Coral's receipt to the bag and handed it to her.

"Thank you." Coral tucked the prescription into her purse and made her way to her car. Perhaps she should call Luke. He was on shift today, and she could give him a heads-up in case of an altercation at the beer store. She tapped in his number and filled him in on what had happened at the pharmacy. After Luke assured her he would head right over, Coral couldn't help herself and drove in that direction too.

Spying the Jeep in front of the establishment, Coral parked at the far end of the lot and leaned over her steering wheel to peer through the large front window of the store. Hopefully, there would be no ugly blow-ups like the one at the drugstore.

A police cruiser pulled into the lot and parked by the main door. Luke exited his vehicle and entered the establishment. How she wished she had an excuse to go inside but figured Luke wouldn't be happy if she did. She was no longer law enforcement, although she desperately wanted to see how the incident played out. Even from a distance, Luke's broad shoulders were noticeable as he stood near the checkouts. His appearance would be intimidating if nothing else.

Coral spied the man in question leaving the store, carrying a case of beer. Luke exited at his heels. Agitated Man did an awkward shuffle through the parking lot while casting repeated looks over his shoulder at the policeman. Luke followed him to his vehicle and when the man slid behind the wheel and slammed his door, he did a rolling motion with his hand at the driver's side window. He conversed with the guy for a few minutes, nodded, and let him go.

Coral slipped from her car and approached Luke. "How did that go? What do you think?"

Luke shrugged. "I asked him if everything was okay. Although a little confused as to why I wanted to know, he said that he was fine. When I questioned him about the injuries to his face, he told me he'd slipped while trying to climb into his Jeep and bashed his face against the running board." Luke squeezed his chin. "His fumbling response did suggest he was fabricating the story, but I didn't have enough to hold him."

"But you didn't believe him?" Coral tapped a finger on her cheek.

"Not exactly, but I guess it could happen. I really had no reason to detain him any longer. He stressed that he was in a hurry, something about having to get back home to feed his girls. His nervous behaviour did raise some flags though."

Coral pursed her lips. "At the pharmacy he also mentioned about getting home to his girls. His actions were very impatient and anxious … near the edge of explosive. That's why I called you."

Luke's countenance was serious. Usually he was so upbeat. Coral was about to ask him if he was having a bad day when she remembered their uncomfortable conversation last night. Luke stared across the parking lot as if he wanted to look anywhere but at her.

After a long stretch of silence, Coral could take the hint. "I'm sorry to take you away from your duties. Maybe the guy truly needed his medication. It seems he is new in the area. He mentioned he recently moved here from Hamilton."

"Never hurts to be cautious. Thanks for the heads-up." Luke's cold response preceded a hurried stride toward his cruiser. Not even a good-bye.

Coral sighed. This was not the Luke she knew, giving her the business-like shoulder. His parting words from yesterday—that he couldn't do this anymore and she needed to decide—flashed through her mind. Jace's similar challenge a few hours ago made her want to groan aloud..

What am I to do?

With a heavy heart, Coral climbed into her vehicle and drove the few blocks to home. As she pulled into the driveway, her stomach growled ferociously. Good thing no one else was in the car with her, or she would have been mighty embarrassed. No doubt her body was protesting since she hadn't eaten much the last few days, distressed over the impossible love triangle she found herself in.

A sudden craving for McDonald's French Fries came over her. *Oh, why not.* One of her favourite snacks might cheer her up. When she arrived at the fast food place, the drive-through line stretched out onto the main road, so she went inside to order. As soon as she opened the door, she recognized the man's irate voice. Not Agitated Man from the pharmacy again. Oh boy. What in the world was he upset about now?

"How could you have run out of Chicken McNuggets? That's insane. I'd like to speak to the manager. This type of service is unacceptable." His hands opened and closed at his sides in a threatening-to-sock-someone-in-the-face manner.

The teenage girl's eyes flashed with fear. "I'll be right back."

Coral's chest muscles grew taught. Should she call Luke again? After the way he'd responded a few minutes ago, that idea didn't hold any appeal. How about Jace? No, she'd carefully monitor the situation and call 911 if warranted. Then it was out of her control as to who would respond. Should she try and deescalate things before they got out of hand?

Coral took a deep breath and approached the man, who was filling a takeout cup at the beverage machine. He took one look at her and his eyes darkened. "Are you following me? Weren't you at the pharmacy a few minutes ago?"

Coral forced a courteous smile to her face. "I'm certainly not following you. We seem to be on the same trajectory with our errands today." She kept her voice low for privacy but more importantly to placate the man. "You seem to be having a bad day. Is there anything I can do to help?"

The man slapped the lid on his frothy soft drink and stared her in the eyes. "As if that concerns you. Mind your own business or you'll be sorry." His challenging glare turned oddly suspicious. "Are you an undercover cop or something?"

Coral tensed. Why would he jump to the undercover cop idea? Had Agitated Man been in trouble with the law before? Was he on the run right now? The average citizen didn't think that way, which suggested a very high possibility.

"Can I help you, sir? I'm Brad. What seems to be the problem?" A short, slim middle-aged man in a signature restaurant uniform stepped toward them. A manager tag was pinned on his shirt.

Agitated Man whirled, took a long draw on his fountain drink, and glowered belligerently at the man in charge. A young mother and her toddler approached the pop machine but held back at the unfolding scene.

"What kind of an establishment are you operating here, Brad? How could you be so short-sighted as to run out of a food option?" His bellowing voice caused many patrons to swivel their heads in the man's direction.

The manager held up a hand toward him. "I'm sorry to disappoint you, sir, and I can assure you that it wasn't an oversight in ordering. The snowstorm on Friday night delayed our shipment. The weather is out of my control. Surely, you understand."

"I may understand, but my twins won't. How do I explain that to them? I can't get them to eat and figured this would tempt them. I've heard most kids like Chicken McNuggets."

Brad offered a conciliatory smile. "How about complimentary ice-cream cones and our free featured toy?"

Agitated Man snarled. "They're too old for toys, and ice cream cones will melt before I get back to Thornton's …" His eyes grew large, and he shoved the straw into his mouth.

Odd. Why had he stopped in the middle of a sentence? Her police radar was bleeping, signifying there was something significant in that slip of the tongue.

"How about coupons for two free cones?" The manager held out his hand as if to shake on the deal.

But the tall, skinny, beat-up looking customer refused the polite gesture. Instead, he took another long draw on his straw. "I want my order free today … all of it. As well as the coupons for free cones."

The manager folded his arms across his chest and studied the man. Almost every eye in the place was zeroed in on the encounter. "That is not ordinarily done, but I'll make an exception in your case. I'll direct my employee that there will be no charge for your order. I think that is more than fair compensation for any inconvenience to you and your wife." Manager Brad's eyes flew to Coral's.

"Oh no, I'm not … we're not together." Coral clasped her purse strap tightly, shaking her head.

"Oh?" Crease lines appeared on Brad's forehead. "Sorry, my mistake."

"Seriously, not my type. This one has been a thorn in my side." Agitated Man sneered as his eyes travelled her body before settling on her face. "Why can't people mind their own business?" His voice rose to a dangerous pitch.

The mother who had been waiting with her child grabbed her daughter's arm and retreated several steps. Coral didn't blame her. This guy was a smoldering gun, cocked full of anger and aggression and ready to explode.

"I'm sorry. I was only trying to help." Coral pivoted on a heel and headed for the shortest line. If only she'd waited in the drive-through instead of coming inside. She'd seen enough of this dude as far as she was concerned.

As she climbed into her vehicle she was thankful that the manager had granted the disgruntled customer's request, essentially deescalating the tension. The tempting aroma of grease and salt filled the interior of her Elantra. Coral couldn't help herself and reached for a fry. Yum. She really was hungry. Before long she found herself digging for the last delicious potato slice, and she hadn't even left the parking lot. As she licked the salt off her fingers, her phone rang out a tune. Wiping her greasy fingers on a napkin, she fished inside her purse and studied the name on the top of the screen. Luke. Hmm. What could he possibly have to say? Was he going to apologize for his silent treatment a few minutes ago? She hit the green phone icon.

"I ran the plates from that man at the beer store. Bingo. You were right in having me check him out. Percy Winkles has been a bad boy. Was only released from prison seven months ago for armed robbery of citizens at ATM machines. He was living in Hamilton until recently when he vacated his apartment, or absconded, to be more accurate. According to the landlord, Mr. Winkles had only paid his first month's rent and nothing for the last six months. The landlord was glad to see him go. If he's in Lighthouse Landing now, he could be a man of concern. Thanks for your keen eye. We'll keep a watch out for him."

Coral scrunched up the greasy napkin and stuffed it inside the paper bag. "I'm glad I felt prompted to check him out and get that license plate number. Oh, and by the way, I ran into him again." She reached for her cup and took a quick sip of her iced-tea.

"What?" Luke's voice rose. "You didn't follow him, did you?"

Coral bit the edge of the straw. She knew where that question had come from. Back when Triple L was on the loose, she'd arranged a tour of the lighthouse and outraged the local police detachment with her meddling. Regardless, they'd discovered a key piece of evidence that night. Coral cringed when she thought about the very serious consequence that followed—a threat on her life. She sighed. That was all in the past. Besides, her interference had been instrumental in catching the murderer, although she still suffered the physical repercussions of the abduction. "Absolutely not. I had a craving for French fries and ran into him at McDonald's. He was giving the staff a hard time because they ran out of Chicken McNuggets. Agitated Man, or Percy, now that I know his name, brought up his girls again, saying he needed food for them."

"That can't be correct. According to the information I found, Mr. Winkles has never married and doesn't have kids. Unless he has children the courts have no records of."

"Apparently these girls weren't young either. When the manager offered him free toys as compensation … oh no." Goosebumps skittered up and down her spine.

"What?"

"I think Percy Winkles may have Gabby and Evangeline." Tingles zipped through her entire body now—the same tingles she got when she was close to solving a case.

"How in the world did you jump to that conclusion? I know you were key in solving the Lighthouse Landing Lament killer, but don't let that go to your head. You ferreted out a nasty character today, and that's all well and good, but to accuse the man of abduction when we don't even know what happened to the girls is crazy. Robbery is his normal MO, not abduction. You are no longer in police work and I suggest you leave it that way."

Ouch. Coral felt as though she'd been slapped, the sensation so real she was surprised her cheek didn't smart … not that she believed Luke would ever hit her. Where in the world was the man she knew? Why was he so angry with her all of a sudden? She set her drink in the cupholder and watched the suspect in question limp toward the main doors, bags and drinks in his hands. "I have very good reason to think like I do. Several things are adding up to make him look suspicious."

"Such as?" Luke challenged.

"His nervous behaviour. His injuries. Perhaps the girls put up a fight. He mentioned twice, once at the pharmacy then at McDonalds, that he needed to get back to his girls to feed them. He said that he *heard* kids liked Chicken McNuggets, not like he *knew* from experience. Judging by what he said to the McDonald's manager when he declined free toys, they weren't young. And he called them twins."

"Are you done now?"

"No." She swallowed against her mounting frustration. "I think you should follow him. He's still here at the fast food place. In fact, he's climbing into his Jeep as we speak. Do you want me to tail him? What could it hurt?"

"Don't you dare! Stay out of police work and stick with your baking." The call ended abruptly.

Double ouch. Coral's jaw clenched. She hadn't expected Luke to be so angry about this. What in the world was going on with him? If he wanted her to decide between him and Jace, he wasn't earning any points in his favour. Nope. No points at all. She tossed the phone inside her purse, grabbed her keys, and started up the engine.

The Jeep Wagoneer sailed past her. Coral tensed, hands gripping the steering wheel tightly. Should she follow him? A huge part of her wanted to, if only to defy Luke. Deliberating, she tapped the steering wheel with her thumbs. Then, not giving herself time to second-guess the decision, she threw her Elantra into drive and tailed him. Agitated guy's right blinker flashed on, signifying he was heading for the highway. She eased up behind him, her thoughts flailing all over the place. Everything in her wanted to trust her instincts—that this man had the twins. Still, even if her senses were bang on and this man had abducted the Fillmore girls, she would hardly be capable of bringing him down. No weapon. And no backup.

Luke's words flashed through her brain—warning her to stay out of police work. She tapped the blinker arm into a downward left position and sighed. Why did everything in her scream that she was making a horrible mistake?

CHAPTER 16

Unpleasant Tasks

The knock brought Jace's head up from the mounds of paperwork in front of him … paperwork involving his new position and extra forms allowing him to be hired temporarily through the month of December. Andrea Miller stood in the doorway. "Officer Kelly? Where's Serg today? I didn't expect to see you at his desk yet, although you're quite the improvement." Her coy smile and batting eyelashes screamed *invitation* ad nauseum. He had to admit that Miller was an extremely attractive woman, but he wasn't interested. She didn't hold a candle to … He shook his head to clear it of that thought. Besides, relationships with coworkers were strictly prohibited. Perhaps she was trying to make a good impression and was being overly friendly. Were small town detachments more lenient when it came to this sort of behaviour? From what he'd observed, Kensington ran a tight ship and Jace doubted he permitted inter-force fraternization.

    Jace did not return her smile. "Serg is off sick today and he asked me to handle things. Can I help you?"

    Seemingly emboldened by the fact the boss was away, she strutted to the side of his desk and ran a manicured fingernail along the edge. "Fresh pot of coffee made. Would you like me to bring you a cup?"

    "Thanks for the offer, but I'm deep in paperwork. I'll help myself when I'm done here." He studied the paper in front of him. When she didn't move, he looked up. "I'm busy, so if you don't mind …"

    "Fine, I can take a hint." She backed up a few steps. "By the way, the Fillmores are here and want to speak to Sergeant Kensington."

    Jace's eyes flew to hers and he let the papers he was holding fall to the desk. "Why didn't you say so up front? Let's not keep them waiting." He straightened in his chair. "Send them in please."

His nerves flashed, first with annoyance at this officer, then with apprehension. Was he up to handling things in Kensington's absence? Especially this heart-wrenching situation?

The distraught couple lingered in the doorway to the office a minute later. Jace got to his feet and waved a hand toward the set of chairs in front of Kensington's desk. "Please have a seat." When they trudged into the room, he proceeded to the door and closed it. "Sergeant Kensington is off today. How are you doing?" Jace rounded the desk again and sat on the edge of the black leather chair. Leaning forward, he rested his elbows on the desk and sank his chin onto his clenched hands.

Ed Fillmore glanced sideways at his wife, who was wiping at puffy eyes with a wad of balled-up tissue. "As good as you can imagine in a situation like this. Any news?" His eyes were large and hopeful.

"I'm sorry." Jace frowned. "Nothing at all. We've been hoping for tips from the public, but so far we've come up blank."

"That's what we feared." Ed fidgeted in his chair. "We have something to tell you that you are most likely not aware of. It may not have any bearing on our missing daughters, but we thought you should know, especially after the odd happening."

Odd happening? Jace cocked his head.

"We adopted Evangeline and Gabby as newborn babies. They are not biologically ours, but we love them as if they were. We've never told the girls. We didn't want them growing up wondering who their real parents were. We thought it would make them insecure and unsettled. Whether it was a mistake on our part remains to be seen. A few months ago, the adoption agency contacted us and said that a man, the biological father, was inquiring about his twin daughters. Of course they didn't tell him anything as we signed a disclosure veto preventing any information from being released."

Brenda Fillmore sniffled, clenching the tissues tightly in her hand. Her lower lip quivered as if she were on the edge of losing it. Jace absorbed this new information. How, if at all, was it connected to the disappearance of the girls?

"We were concerned at first about the biological father's quest, thinking that our daughters' lives were about to be turned upside down. But we dismissed it when we didn't hear anything more."

Brenda clutched her husband's forearm. "Tell him about the vehicle."

He nodded at his wife. "I'm sorry that we hadn't thought to bring this up when we talked to you and the sergeant the other day." He took a deep breath. "It may be nothing, but we noticed a gold-coloured Jeep—an older model, not sure of the make—driving slowly by the farm fairly often, say several times a week. It made us a little uncomfortable, but we never felt led to report it. Until now."

Jace mulled over this latest bit of information as the possibility of an abduction now seemed more plausible. Could it involve the biological father? Could he have somehow discovered where his daughters lived? He bit his bottom lip. What would be the likelihood of that happening?

Ed reached for his wife's hand and squeezed it. "When you put those two things together, Brenda and I are worried they may be connected."

"And rightly so. You may be onto something there." He tapped his fingers on the desk. "If you are correct in your assumptions, that maybe the biological father abducted your girls, then hopefully they will not be harmed. Perhaps he was desperate to have them back in his life."

Brenda's eyes widened. "I hadn't thought of it that way. If that's the case, we have hope that they are alive and well somewhere, not …" Her breath hitched.

Jace's pulse quickened with resolve. The longer the girls were missing, the more urgent and complicated the case became. It was good in the sense that their frozen bodies hadn't been discovered in a farmer's field, but bad because the abduction theory seemed more likely now.

"Can I get you anything? Water? Coffee? A soft drink?" Jace offered, as he got to his feet, bracing himself on the top of the desk.

The couple shook their heads in unison. "No thanks. We have to get back to the farm." Ed rose and held out a hand to his wife. She wobbled unsteadily after she stood, probably weak from exhaustion, worry, and lack of sleep.

Jace opened the door to the office. "Don't lose hope. We've got officers on the case even as we speak."

Ed nodded. "We've seen patrol cars often on our road and heard the helicopter circling this morning."

"We're hoping for a tip from the public, as the local news is reporting the story several times a day. In fact, it's being broadcast on all the major news outlets in Ontario. Even some American border cities are picking up the story. And Customs has been notified." Jace grasped Ed's shoulder. "We'll let you know the minute we learn anything new."

"Thank you." Mr. Fillmore's voice was solemn as he led his wife down the hallway toward the lobby.

Jace propped a shoulder against the doorframe to the office, his mind swirling with this latest information until the phone on Kensington's desk rang. He hurried to answer the call. "Officer Kelly." It was Kensington himself, although he sounded like a croaking frog, inquiring about updates on the Fillmore Twins' Case. Jace filled him in on the information the Fillmores had just provided him. "By the way, you sound terrible, boss. Hope you're feeling better soon." Jace listened as Kensington regaled him with tales of his woes—that his wife was babying him too much, making him drink lemon tea with honey and rubbing his chest with a natural concoction that stank like a moldy basement. When he finished, Jace laughed and wished his boss well before hanging up.

A melancholy cloud hung over Jace as he wondered what it might be like to have someone taking care of him like that. Would he ever have a woman in his life? Coral's face flashed through his mind and he winced. Things were not great between them right now, and he didn't know how to make them right. Or if he even could. He recalled Kensington's advice the last time they'd talked, right here in this very office. *Have you told her how you feel?*

Yes. He had told her Sunday right after church—that the kiss Saturday morning was perfect, completing him and filling him with joy. And then she had admitted that Luke and her had grown close. Jace raked a hand through his hair and paced the length of the office, praying as he strode. *God, I don't know what to do. Please help me. I believe that Coral has to decide. Give me strength to wait patiently and grace and mercy to work with Luke Degroot. To treat him as fairly as every other officer. He seems like a fine, upstanding man. I don't want to interfere if Coral's meant to be with him.* His throat thickened. *But I love her, God. I truly do. If Luke is her choice, please take these strong feelings away from me.*

His cell vibrated in his pocket and he retrieved it. His pulse quickened as her name appeared on the screen. Coral needed to see him. His palms grew clammy. Was this good news or bad? Had she made her decision already? Either way, he had to face it like a man.

Jace locked Kensington's office and approached the main desk in the lobby. He left a message with Brittany the operator, saying that he would be taking his break across the street at the café. If they needed him, they could refer any calls to his cell. He donned his winter attire, opened the door, and saw Luke tromping through the parking lot toward the main doors of the police station. Jace nodded. "Morning, Degroot. Anything to report? Anything new on the Fillmore Case?"

"No, sir. The copter is out searching fields along Concession 7 now that the snow has melted considerably." Luke submitted the report rather blankly. "Yesterday was fairly quiet too, other than a complaint from a shopper about a worrisome customer at the pharmacy."

"Oh? How did that go? Anything to be concerned about? Did it get resolved?" Jace zipped up his parka and donned his gloves.

"All taken care of. The customer was upset about a medication he needed that had no refills. I think it was an over-reaction by the complainant who, as far as I could tell should have minded her own business." Luke's words carried disdain. Perhaps he was having a bad day. Did it have anything to do with Coral? Or the fact that Jace was back in town for good? Maybe he was as worried about the decision Coral would make as he was.

Jace nodded. "I'll be back shortly. I'm …" He was about to tell Luke where he was headed and thought better of it. "Any problems, call my cell." Jace strode thought the parking lot, feeling Luke's eyes on his back. Oh well, it wasn't a secret that he was going to Coral's Muffin Cup Café. It was a well known fact that she did have the best coffee in town, not to mention the desserts were pretty spectacular too. Besides, she'd contacted him. He chuckled to himself as he remembered his first visit with Coral last September as she tried her best to make a sweet-lover out of him. He had to admit her caramel-pecan coffee cake was delicious. But truly, sweets were not his thing. Except of course for butter tarts.

She met him at the door, her features drawn and pinched. "Do you have a minute? Something's bothering me. In fact, I've been wrestling with it all night. I need to talk to you."

Oh boy. Was this it? Was she dumping him? Choosing Luke over him?

Jace wrestled out of his coat and hung it on the hook behind the café door. When he turned, Coral was approaching the booth, two mugs in hand. He watched her set the mugs on the table.

Suddenly his desire for coffee fled. He took a seat across from her and stared at the steaming mug. "Thanks for the coffee."

"I had an interesting day yesterday. To be honest, I can't stop thinking about it and I need to vent."

Jace didn't know whether to be relieved or not. He wasn't sure where this conversation was headed but hopefully away from him. The aroma of coffee wafted up his nostrils and tempted him. He gave in, reached for the mug, took a sip, and sighed. Coral truly made the best coffee around. And he'd tried a lot of coffee in his time, especially with the large variety of shops in Toronto. He'd have to ask her one day what her secret was.

"I was in the pharmacy yesterday and there was a very agitated man ahead of me in line at the prescription counter. When he couldn't get his meds, he became belligerent and intimidated the pharmacist. When she threatened to call the police, he turned to leave. I gasped when I saw his face. He was a mess, like he'd been in a fight. He sported an injured eye and broken nose. He complained that he needed to get home to his girls and that the beer store better be open, or someone was going to pay. His speech and actions bordered on dangerous, so I followed him and took down the license plate as well as the make and model of his car. I called it in because his behaviour warranted it. Then, I followed the man to the beer store where I remained in my car and watched as Luke talked with him. Afterward, Luke didn't seem too concerned."

Jace sat up a little straighter as Luke's words about a nosy complainant rang through his thoughts. Could he possibly have been referring to Coral? If so, he seemed none too pleased with her.

"Afterwards, I had a craving for McDonald's French Fries. The drive-through was extremely backed-up, so I went inside the restaurant, only to find that same man in there. In fact, I heard him first, yelling at the young girl at the counter. He was upset that there were no Chicken McNuggets for his girls. To make a long story short, the manager talked with him and calmed him down, then agreed to give Agitated Man free meals after the man insisted on them."

"Okay. I'm not sure where you're going with this yet. Agitated Man sounds a little troubled, but maybe he was having a bad day." Jace took another swallow of the brew. The coffee tasted better than he ever remembered because Coral wasn't dumping him … at least at the moment.

"Wait until you hear the rest. While I was enjoying the fries in my car, Luke called me. He'd run a check on Agitated Man's license plate and discovered some very disturbing information. The man's name is Percy Winkles, and he was released from prison seven months ago after being convicted of the armed robbery of several customers at ATM machines. Apparently, he recently fled his apartment in Hamilton after failing to pay his rent. Luke thanked me for my observations, which gave them a heads-up that this man was in our area."

Jace's thoughts immediately flew to Big Dutch. Why hadn't Luke Degroot filed a report about this man and informed the detachment? Disquiet settled over Jace. He'd have to deal with Luke the moment he left Coral's café. "I see your criminal senses were vibrating. And apparently they were right on. Good job." He managed a crooked smile, which she didn't seem to even notice.

"As I was talking to Luke, it hit me." Her eyes grew large as saucers and her words came quickly.

"What hit you?"

Coral slapped the table as her voice rose excitedly. "It was a combination of a lot of things starting with the man's nervous behaviour. Then his injuries, which he justified to Luke as slipping when he climbed into his Jeep and smacking his face off his running boards. Followed by his continual reference to getting food for his girls, which he later changed to twins. He declined toys because he said the girls weren't little. If you add it all up and combine it with his criminal background, I can't shake the idea that he abducted Evangeline and Gabby." Coral clasped her hands together and pressed them against her mouth. "If only Luke had listened to me."

Jace choked on a mouthful of coffee. He coughed, set his mug down, and held up a hand. "Wait a minute. Back up. Did you say this man drove a Jeep?" Jace coughed some more as he slapped at his chest.

Coral nodded.

"What colour was it?" His voice was raspy. Drat! That coffee had gone down the wrong hole. He hated when that happened.

"Bronze or gold. I can never tell the difference between the two. It was an older model, a rusted Jeep Wagoneer."

A sick feeling coursed through Jace. He cleared his voice. And cleared it again in a desperate attempt to get enough oxygen. "And you said he called his girls twins?"

"Yes. I tried to get Luke to follow the man. If only he had, we may have found them. If I was wrong, what harm could it have caused?"

"Exactly. I'm with you. Why wouldn't Luke listen to your suggestion?"

Coral's eyes shifted toward her clenched hands. "I'm not sure. He seemed very annoyed with me. His words hurt. In fact, he told me to stay in the kitchen, that I was no longer in police work."

Ouch. Jace could almost feel Coral's pain. Despite that, he gloated a little. Perhaps this would turn her affections away from Big Dutch and onto him. Then he chided himself for such a thought. The important thing was finding the twins. He recalled the conversation he'd just had with the Fillmores. They had mentioned a Jeep of similar colour going by their place often. What if she was right? If they were connected, he now had the name of a possible suspect. He'd have to contact the adoption agency and find out who the biological father was.

"What are you thinking? Am I crazy? Grasping at straws? It's not like I set out to get involved in the missing twins' case. It just happened."

Jace wrestled with how much he should tell her. What if she was correct? Had this man Percy Winkles abducted the Fillmore women as she'd imagined? Was he their biological father? Or was all of this a weird coincidence and totally unrelated? Yet Coral seemed to have an inner sense about things when it came to solving crimes. He recalled her insistence that they check the dumpster behind the Riddells' cottage when they were in the middle of the Bacon murder investigation last year. Her instincts were correct when she discovered a backpack inside that led to the identity of the husband as murderer.

"I don't think you're crazy at all." He reached across the table and covered her hands with his. "You've given me key information, especially about the vehicle and the man's name, but I'm not permitted to say anything else. It's highly possible that you're on the right track. If only Luke had tailed him."

Jace finished his coffee and got to his feet. "I'm acting sergeant today as Kensington is off sick. I have things to take care of and need to get back to the station." Should he mention that he was relieved he was still in the running for her heart?

As he donned his coat, he fought the desire to pull her into his arms and kiss her like he had Saturday morning. He tamped down the urge and kept it to a smile and a goodbye.

As he clomped through the café parking lot, a feeling of dread coursed through him—dread at dealing with Degroot's actions and dread at the missing twins' situation. Had Coral's suspicions been correct? Had the women been abducted by Percy Winkles in his bronze or gold Jeep Wagoneer? Were they too late? He sincerely prayed that wasn't the case. He entered the police station lobby and found Degroot, his elbow leaning on the counter, smiling at Officer Miller. She had a hand on his shoulder, and he appeared to be enjoying it a little too much. If only Coral could see him now. To give Luke credit, Miller was an obnoxious flirt.

A feeling of anxiety came over Jace as unpleasant duties piled up. He wasn't sure he was going to like this new role of sergeant and all the responsibilities that came with it. But wait. Despite the fact it wouldn't be easy, he knew he had it in him. He'd often been reprimanded in his previous position for ordering his coworkers around. Jace clamped his lips together as embarrassment flooded through him. That was the past. God had done amazing things in his heart since then. Now he was in a position where he could right the wrongs of this world and do it legitimately.

God help me to always be fair and wise.

Today's unpleasantries began with the man standing in front of him. He slipped out of his boots. "Degroot? In my office now."

CHAPTER 17

Guilt and Love

Percy plunked the cold burgers down in front of the twins. "Eat up. There's nothing else in the house except for a box of stale soda crackers and a case of beer. And you have no idea of the hassle I went through to get these. I ordered Chicken McNuggets for you, because all kids like those, but can you believe McDonald's was out?"

Evangeline pushed her burger aside. "How old do you think we are? Quit calling us kids. I wasn't hungry last night and I'm not hungry now. Why don't you just let us go?"

"It's your choice to decline the food, but if you don't start eating something soon, you're going to get weak and sick and … I can't lose you. Not after I finally found you both." His eyes darted from Evangeline's to Gabby's and back again.

"Are you going to start on that kick again? That you're our father? Because no matter what you say, we won't believe you." Evangeline pounded a fist on the table.

Man, she was a feisty one. Not like her sister Gabby, who played with the edge of the hamburger wrapper, her hand visibly shaking. "Try this one on. You were born June 4th, 1998 in Port Hope, Ontario."

Gabby's eyes almost bulged out of her head. "How do you know our birthdays?"

"How wouldn't I know the date of your births? I was there, silly girl." Percy stroked Gabby's hair and she sank lower in her chair. "You were the cutest little peanuts. Sadly, I was only allowed to hold you briefly then it was over. I never saw you again."

"Anyone can find that information about our birthdays. Perhaps you creeped our Facebook accounts." Evangeline fired back at him.

"Facebook? I don't visit those social media sites. In fact, I don't even own a smart phone or a computer. I know the date of your birth because I was there, with your mother." Percy frowned. "Evangeline, you were born first and weighed five pounds three ounces. Gabby came three minutes later and weighed five pounds on the nose. Everything went downhill after that. I wanted to keep you, but your mother didn't. We were both teenagers and Bethany felt she was unable to care for you. It's true, we were young, still in high-school with no way to support you, but I vowed to quit school and find a full-time job to provide for my family. However, Bethany wouldn't agree and unfortunately I lost the battle. Your mother not only put you up for adoption against my wishes, she moved away, and I never heard from her again." His voice cracked. "I truly loved you and wanted you. You've got to believe me."

"Did you get dropped on your head? We've grown up on our family's chicken farm outside of Lighthouse Landing all of our lives. Surely, our parents would have told us if we were adopted. If you were truly our father, you would want the best for us. Why would you steal us from the only home and family we've ever known?" Evangeline was no longer barking at him but wailing. Tears were spilling out of Gabby's eyes too.

Great. He never knew how to handle female tears.

Percy grabbed at his hair. "Because I wanted what was due me. My daughters were snatched from my life and I had no control over it. How do you think I felt?"

"So you're paying us back for something we also had no control over either? We were babies. If what you're saying is true, why not go through the legal system and ask for visiting rights?" Gabby whimpered.

"I tried that. I got absolutely nowhere. They wouldn't divulge the information. Apparently your adoptive parents signed a disclosure veto that blocks any adoption or birth information, even though you are over the age of eighteen."

Evangeline shot to her feet, swiping at tears. "You can't keep us here forever. You know we'll eventually escape and get help."

Percy smirked. "Yeah well, good luck with that. Even if you were to get out of the building, you're in the heavily forested and remote Thornton's Swamp. The nearest neighbour is at least a half hour's drive away. And winter is settling in. How far do you think you'd get in those skimpy little elf costumes?"

"We could try. We have our coats and boots." Gabby's voice quivered. "It's inhumane what you've done to us. You can't keep us locked up in a small room forever."

Percy let the handful of curls fall from between his fingers. "How well I know you have your boots." He tenderly touched his nose. "I do feel bad about keeping you locked up though." He paced the small kitchen. "Tell you what. I'll offer you a deal. When I'm home, you can have freedom to roam the place. That way, every time one of you needs to use the washroom, I don't have to unlock the door. What do you think? Will you behave yourselves?"

"Of course we will. Won't we, Gabby?" Evangeline tilted her head toward the frying pan sitting on the stove.

But Percy had followed her gaze. "After I hide this." He picked up the utensil. "So, I'll need you to sashay yourselves back down the hall and into your room temporarily, then I promise I'll let you back out."

Gabby got to her feet and stood beside her sister while Percy shooed the girls out of the kitchen and into the hallway with the scratched Teflon pan. Then he reached for the key behind the bird book in the living area. When he realized they'd seen his hiding spot, he cursed. What an idiot he was sometimes.

"Don't you have to go to work or something? How will you feed us or take care of us properly? Have you thought about that?" Evangeline's voice had lost its sassiness.

"I quit, although they don't know it yet." His smirk was cocky. "They think I'm sick. I wasn't appreciated there anyway. I worked like a dog and all I heard was, Percy the washrooms need cleaning. Percy wipe down those tables. Percy scrub the floor. Sheesh. You'd think I was the only employee. Besides, I have a little bit tucked away, so no need to worry your pretty little heads."

"If that's the case, why are there only stale soda crackers in the house?" Evangeline thrust her chin forward.

"What's with all these questions? Because I don't like to cook. I'm a fast food junky. Does that satisfy your smart mouth? You are just like your mother."

"I have a question." Gabby's voice squeaked like a timid little mouse. "How did you find us if you said the documents were sealed? How do you know we're the daughters you've been looking for?"

Swinging the pan along behind them, he urged them into their bedroom. Once they were inside, Percy let the frying pan dangle at his left side as he blocked the doorway. "Now that's an intelligent question. Naturally, one of my kids would have my smarts." He puffed out his chest. "It's sort of a miracle. I think God loves me after all." His cackle carried a mocking edge. "It's like He led me right to you. I was driving through the area one day and stopped in at the coffee shop that eventually hired me. You were both there at a table by the window. As soon as I saw you I knew you were my girls."

Evangeline's eyes narrowed. "How in the world would you know that? You hadn't seen us since the day we were born, so you say."

Percy reached out a hand toward her face. She cringed. "Don't touch me. Get away."

"I'm not going to hurt you. You have her birthmark … the café au lait spot on your chin, in the exact place your mother had it." He pointed at the mark.

Evangeline touched her chin with a finger and cast a worried glance at Gabby.

"You both are the spitting image of Bethany." He set the frying pan on the tile floor and fished his wallet from his pocket. "I'll prove it to you." He held up a faded photo with torn edges toward them.

Both girls stepped a little closer and stared at the picture. Gabby gasped and covered her mouth. "Not only does she look like us, she's got the same mark on her chin as you, Evangeline. Is it possible?"

Evangeline didn't speak, rather looked like she might vomit.

"You finally believe me, don't …"

Evangeline charged toward him. Her eyes fixated to the frying pan on the floor. Before she could reach it, Percy stepped a foot into the pan and grabbed both of her arms. "Will you ever stop? No way are you inflicting more pain on your father." Percy snickered. "Your feistiness reminds me of your mother. She really was a pain. It's probably for the best we never ended up together." He gave her a gentle nudge backwards. "Why can't you accept your fate like your sister here?"

"I have news for you," Evangeline's nostrils flared. "Gabby is not the shy, quiet girl you think she is. Her patience has a limit, and when she blows, you'd better not be anywhere nearby."

Percy's eyes twinkled at the challenge. "Is that a fact? Thanks for the warning. I'll keep that in mind. Time to hide the frying pan and key. Then maybe I'll think of letting you out for a few hours. Or maybe I won't. Not after the way you've been treating your father."

The heavy metal rock song blared from his pocket.

"Where's the music coming from?" Evangeline's brow crinkled.

"That's my phone and it's probably work looking for me. Ha. Not going back to that place ever again, although they do have great coffee. Come to think of it, I heard of another place in town, Coral's Muffin Cup Café, that is rumoured to have an even better brew. Perhaps I'll pay a visit there one of these days since I can't show my face at Timmy's anymore."

Gabby's face suddenly lit up. "Please. They have the best date squares in the whole world and I'm really hungry now. I could go for one of those and some coffee. Both of us could, couldn't we, Evangeline?"

"Did you just wink at your sister? What's with that?" Percy pursed his lips.

"I have something in my eye." Gabby gently massaged her eyelid.

"Fine. You I trust. Your sister I don't. If it'll make you eat, I'll gladly drive into town and pick up some coffee and date squares for all of us. Unfortunately, that means you'll be locked in here for another few hours. Anyone need to use the little girl's room first?" When he was met with silence, he reversed into the hallway and locked the door.

As he drove into town, he had a sneaking suspicion his twins were up to something. But he needn't worry. They'd have a monumental task, getting one step ahead of him. His hands shook as he gripped the wheel. Drat! The beer he'd consumed before bed had gotten him through the night, but the effects were wearing off and he'd forgotten to call his psychiatrist for that much needed refill.

He pulled over to the side of the road, threw old Betsy into park, and punched in the number. He sighed with relief after the doctor promised to fax his refill to town within the next hour. Phew! Two birds with one stone. Things were beginning to look up for him. Maybe today would be a good day.

A sinking feeling came over him when he realized whose home he sat in front of. He'd have to remember to drive a different way in the future. The large sign announcing the Fillmore Chicken Farm haunted him. He glanced toward the well-kept farmhouse and large property, desperately hoping no one had noticed his Jeep. Not that anyone would be able to connect it to the missing twins.

Be sure your sins will find you out.

The prison pastor's words disturbed his thoughts, making him even more anxious than he already was. He wished he'd never heard them. Why wouldn't they go away? Despite the fact that he'd been arrested in the past, resulting in his seven-year prison term, he didn't believe the pastor—that God had allowed him to be apprehended. He was unlucky, like he had been all his life. Nothing ever went his way.

Despite his mocking comment to the girls a few minutes ago about God leading him to find them, could it be true? Surely God wouldn't condone kidnapping. He couldn't shake the guilt. Perhaps he'd made a big mistake in snatching the girls, his girls, from a home where they were not only loved, but cared for far beyond what he could ever provide. Wasn't love the most important thing? He knew from the meager way he'd lived up until now that you truly didn't need all the material things everyone thought you did.

Checking his mirror, he eased off the gravel shoulder and pulled back onto Concession 7. He swallowed against the lump forming in his throat as he recalled pouring out his heart to that man. Pastor Elliott had told him that God loved him. He found that hard to believe. Nope. Not him. God didn't love him. Neither did anyone else. Maybe one day his twins would come to understand that he abducted them because he loved them. Dare he believe that perhaps they would even love him in return?

CHAPTER 18

Narrow Misses

Coral squeezed out the letter *y* in blue icing on the top of the vanilla-frosted cake then studied her creation. A sense of accomplishment flooded over her. She really did love baking. The *Happy 40th Wedding Anniversary* cake was a request from Sylvia Kensington for her and her husband's anniversary tomorrow. Coral sighed. What would it be like to be married for forty years? Even if she got married tomorrow, she'd be in her late seventies by the time she celebrated that many years. *If* she ever married. At the rate things were going, it didn't seem likely at all.

She washed her sticky hands at the sink, then dried them on a tea towel. The bell jingled, signifying a customer, so she removed her apron, tossed it onto the counter, and hurried through the kitchen. She froze at the sight of the man in her café. Judging by his fiery glare he seemed none too pleased to see her either.

"You've got to be kidding me." He slapped a hand on the glass counter-top. "Not you again. Twice yesterday, now today? Are you spooking me or something? Is there someone else who can wait on me?"

"Nope. I run a one-woman operation." Coral slowly approached the display case, her mind racing with where she'd left her cell phone last. "I can assure you that I have no desire to haunt you. Besides, you entered *my* café today—need I remind you." She forced a smile to her face. "Maybe we got off to a rocky start." She extended a hand across the counter. "I'm Coral the owner and you are?"

"Percy Winkles," He ignored her outstretched hand.

"Nice to meet you, Percy. How are those girls of yours? Were they happy with the burgers?" Was the smile she'd plastered on—in juxtaposition to the worry and mistrust swirling inside—fooling him?

He studied her for a moment, his eyes narrowed. If he only knew that she'd recorded his license plate number, followed him to the beer store, and suspected him of abducting the Fillmore twins. Then his cynicism would definitely be justified. The black ring around his eye was very pronounced now and his twisted nose was swollen. "My girls are fine. Apparently they're craving your coffee and date squares. Believe me, that's the only reason for this visit."

Coral's mind raced. She had been correct in her assumption that his girls couldn't be that young, especially if they liked coffee. And now she knew that they had been in her café before. How many youngish-but-old-enough-to-drink-coffee sets of twins had been here in the last year? Her heart rate picked up. Only one that she could think of. "Always good to hear that people are enjoying my desserts. How many squares would you like?"

He peered into the display case. "Half a dozen." His voice was gruff, and his breath reeked—the putrid odour puffing across the glass counter top and assaulting her nostrils.

"Coming right up." Coral reached for a pastry box and the pair of tongs, happy to turn away from the smell. "You can help yourself to the drinks. The coffee is over there." She nodded in the direction of the station.

The man shuffled to the counter, still favouring his left foot. A few minutes later he approached, juggling three coffees. She grabbed a cardboard takeout tray and set the drinks inside. "That will be twenty dollars."

His eyes shot wide open. "Mighty pricey, don't you think? Are those pastries lined with gold filling?"

"I'm sorry. Gluten-free baking is expensive as the ingredients are very pricey."

A scowl twisted across his face, but he shrugged. "Fine. Gotta make my girls happy." He reached into his pocket, retrieved a wallet, and pulled out a twenty-dollar bill.

"Are you new to the area? I am. I moved here last April. I had no idea of the type of weather Lighthouse Landing received in the winter. That snowsquall the other day was awful, don't you agree?" Coral handed him the receipt.

"Has anyone ever told you that you talk too much?" His eyes darkened as he grabbed the coffee tray and pastry box and staggered across the café. He shoved against the door with a shoulder, then hurried through the parking lot.

Coral cringed at the man's nastiness. If he was responsible for the abduction of the Fillmore twins, the quicker they could discover where he had them, the better. Desperate to inform Jace, she ran into the kitchen. Where in the world had she left her cell? Coral shoved containers of flour and sugar out of the way, frantic to find it. It was not like her to misplace her only means of communication.

He's getting away. Exhaling in frustration, Coral raced to lock her café door. She'd have to follow him herself. Charging through her apartment side door, she hopped into her vehicle and started the engine. The Jeep was turning right from her parking lot, onto the main road. Scanning both directions, she backed down her driveway and followed as closely as possible.

Would Mr. Winkles notice her in his rear-view mirror? If so, would he stop and confront her? Luke would not be happy at all with her impulsive interference. Hopefully he wouldn't find out. Was she doing the right thing? What if Percy led her straight to the girls? Then what? She had no weapon and no phone to call for the police. Coral bit her lip. What in the world was she getting herself into? She shoved back her shoulders. It didn't matter. She had to try to find them. She had to. Those intuitive tingles were zapping through her at top speed and she felt strongly that this was the man who'd kidnapped the twins.

Oops. She'd gotten too close. Her eyes connected with Mr. Wide-Eyed Winkles' wary ones when she had to hurry through an amber stoplight in order to not lose him. What would he do?

When he fish-tailed down the road, tires squealing, Coral cringed. What a terribly foolish thing to do and right in downtown Lighthouse Landing. What if a child ran into the road? Coral didn't speed up. Police chases were very dangerous and highly frowned upon. Not to mention, she wasn't in law enforcement anymore.

No!

A jolt of fear stabbed her in the chest as a silver-haired man, pushing a walker, stepped out from between two parked cars and began crossing the street. Right in front of her.

Screaming, she slammed on the brakes. Inches from the man, her car slid to a halt. Coral pressed a palm to her thudding heart. Thank goodness she'd decided not to get involved in a high-speed chase with the Jeep. If she had … She clutched the steering wheel tightly. She couldn't even allow herself to think that horrifying thought. As the adrenaline coursing through her waned, her head flopped against the wheel as her heart rate attempted to recover its normal rhythm.

After waiting for the old man, who seemed oblivious to his near-death experience, she blew out a breath and scanned the road in front of her. Not a sign of the Jeep.

Turning into a business parking lot, she drove down Main Street to her bakery. When she entered her kitchen, she spied her phone sitting on the ledge above the sink. She slapped her hands on her hips, feeling like a clumsy failure. She'd have to make a mental note to always place the phone in the same spot each time so she could find it in a hurry, if need be. Although it was probably too late, she punched in her passcode and hit the contact number for Jace.

"Can you explain to me why I don't have a proper report about yesterday's citizen complaint call concerning an unruly customer at the pharmacy and beer store?" Jace's phone rang but he ignored it.

Officer Degroot shifted on the black plastic chair across from Jace's desk. "I … just hadn't gotten around to doing it yet."

"Why? Were there other calls or duties that kept you from filing the information?" Jace organized a stack of papers and set them on a corner of the desk.

Officer Degroot frowned. "The incident was overblown and not worth a response. By the time I drove back from the beer store it was almost five o'clock. Miller needed help with a case she's working on, so I thought that was more important. And my shift ended at seven so …"

Jace studied Luke carefully. "Did you run plates on a Jeep Wagoneer or did you not?"

One of Degroot's eyebrows shot up. "I did. How did you know that?"

"What did you discover?" Jace steepled his fingers at his nose.

"That the owner's name was Percy Winkles, and he has a prison record for armed robbery of ATM customers." He paused, his expression morphing annoyed. "I assume you talked to Coral."

"You assume correctly. She was concerned that this man may have the missing Fillmore twins. With everything you learned, why did you not agree to her suggestion to follow the man?"

Luke scowled. "No offense, sir, but she is no longer in law enforcement. The probability of the man being behind the twins' abductions is so ludicrously minimal based on her observations— that he seemed nervous, had facial injuries, and talked about getting home to his girls. How in the world does that connect him to the case?"

Jace barely resisted the urge to smack his forehead. "Have we not asked for the public's help in locating the women?"

"Well … yes."

"Didn't you discover the man had a criminal record?"

"Yes." Luke cleared his throat.

"Two reasons right there to at least follow up on the idea. What could it hurt?"

"When you put it that way, nothing, I guess." A red flush crept up the man's neck.

Jace picked up a pen and tapped it against his desk. "There are a few other reasons that pursuing Percy Winkles may have been a very wise thing to do. Ed and Brenda Fillmore paid me a visit this morning and reported seeing a gold, older-model, Jeep Wagoneer driving slowly by their farm for the past few weeks."

Luke blanched and held up his palms. "Whoa. Hardly my fault as I didn't have access to that information yet."

"In addition, they informed me that their daughters were adopted as babies. Apparently their biological father has recently been inquiring about visiting rights but was declined because of a non-disclosure clause." Jace's phone rang. He ignored it again.

"Let me guess. The biological father's name is Percy Winkles." Luke's complexion paled even further.

"We'll know as soon as you do your job and contact the adoption agency in Port Hope."

Luke shot to his feet. "On it." He turned to leave then stopped abruptly. "Sorry about the way I handled Coral's request. I seriously didn't think it was connected in the slightest. And Miller's case seemed pressing."

"What case would that be?" Jace folded his arms across his chest and stared at Officer Degroot.

"Unimportant now, sir. I'll file that report from yesterday's incident right after I contact the adoption agency. Am I dismissed?"

His phone rang again. *Sheesh! Why won't my phone stop ringing?* He held up a finger toward Luke. "Hold on." Jace yanked the device from his shirt pocket. When he saw the name on the screen he tensed. Coral had tried to contact him three times in short succession. Was something wrong? He hit the phone icon. "Kelly." His mouth fell open as he listened to her account of everything that had just happened. "Thanks. Getting right on it."

Jace shoved the phone into his pocket and stood. "Degroot, get in your patrol car pronto. You'll be searching for that Jeep Wagoneer again. Apparently, the man was in Coral's bakery just now, and left town at a high rate of speed, heading north. She tried to follow him but to no avail. I'll handle the adoption agency. Take Newton with you. I'll send Carlisle out with Jenkins too. The more eyes on the road, the better. Take a swing by the Fillmore Chicken Farm also."

"On it, sir." Luke headed for the door.

"Watch out for Miller."

Luke whirled, his hand on the doorknob. "Pardon?"

"She's spinning a web. Don't get caught."

"No offense, but I've worked with her for a number of years and know her better than you. Not my type. Not interested. And not on the job." Luke's voice was laced with disdain.

"That's not what I witnessed this morning, and it will be my business in a few short weeks. Any hint of a relationship and I'll put an end to it pronto."

"Go ahead. Ending relationships is what you do best." Luke opened the door and stormed down the hallway.

Jace leaned forward, his palms on Kensington's desk, as Luke's derisive words walloped him hard. Is that how he was perceived by Big Dutch? A relationship wrecker? Wait a minute. He'd known Coral first. In fact, he was in love with her several months before Luke came on the scene. All the same, a heaviness settled over him at Luke's caustic comment. Perhaps it was best to step back now—leave Lighthouse Landing and return to Toronto. If Coral didn't give him an answer soon, that's exactly what he'd do.

He plunked down on Kensington's office chair and picked up the phone. "Brittany. I need you to patch me through to the Port Hope Adoption Agency. And I need it yesterday. Drop whatever you're doing. It's urgent. Thanks." He ended the call and waited about five minutes until his phone rang. Officer Kelly identified himself to the representative at the adoption agency and explained the urgent reason for his call. He was put on hold for another few minutes until finally the woman supplied him with the information needed. He thanked her immensely and hung up the phone.

Percy Winkles was indeed the Fillmore twins' biological father. Coral's hunch may be correct after all.

CHAPTER 19

Ethereal Feelings and Biological News

Percy stared into his rear-view mirror and let out a loud whoop. He'd finally ditched that pesky woman. What was she, anyway, some kind of wannabe cop? And being smarter than the average bear, he'd driven one concession past 7 and taken a parallel sideroad. No more travelling past the Fillmore property, even if it took him fifteen minutes out of his way. Much too risky.

Satisfied that no one was following him, he pulled onto the shoulder, shoved the transmission into park, and idled the vehicle. With shaky hands, he removed the lid of the prescription bottle and tapped two more pills onto his palm. That nosy woman had negated the effect of the first two he'd taken at the pharmacy. The extra meds might make him drowsy, but there was something about that Coral woman. For some reason, she set his nerves on edge, more so than they already were. Was she onto him? Whenever her eyes locked onto his, it was as if his soul was exposed or something. How in the world did she do that?

Be sure your sins will find you out.

Percy slammed the back of his head against the headrest. No. Why wouldn't those voices stop harassing him? His grip on the steering wheel tightened. Harassment was too gentle a word. It was more like torture. An odd feeling came over him suddenly, as if a blanket of peace and incredible love surrounded his vehicle. His soul told him it was God reaching out to him. It was so other-worldly he couldn't explain it any other way. But he balked at that idea, chalking it up to the pills' effects. Percy let go of the wheel with one hand to massage a sore spot on his skull … probably from yanking out too much hair. His pastor had warned him that God loved him and was pursuing him—that he should stop running and accept His incomparable love.

Was God after him? The pastor's words ricocheted through his mind. Pastor Elliott had said that he would be praying for him every day, despite the fact that Percy told him not to bother. But every wrong thing he'd ever done, accompanied by this powerful, ethereal, incomprehensible feeling, jelled together to make him want to sob like a baby. He pressed his trembling lips together. What was happening to him? Was he falling apart? Could the pastor's words be true—that God loved him? But no one had ever loved him. He'd been rejected by his own parents and floated through the foster system, always feeling outside the family unit that took him in. He hung his head, overwhelmed with emotion. Was he that unlovable? He had so much love inside him to give but no one to give it to.

Until now. He sat up suddenly, resolve coursing through him as bitterness rose and the supernatural feeling left. God didn't love him. He wished he'd never met Pastor Elliott. He checked his mirror and pulled onto the gravel sideroad. *Better get home to my girls.* It was only a matter of time before they understood how much he loved them. Dare he hope that one day they might even love him back?

Soon, he was bouncing along the rutted, snowy, muddy access road leading to his temporary home at the visitor centre. When he arrived, he stepped out of the Jeep and surveyed it. Old Betsy was a splattered, ugly mess. He'd need to give his beloved vehicle a bath soon. Maybe he'd run it through the car wash in town. Then reality hit. He really couldn't show his face, or his truck, in Lighthouse Landing anymore as he highly suspected they were onto him. Or at least they would be after that snooping bakery chef went to the police, which he was pretty sure she would.

He set the coffee and desserts on the kitchen table, retrieved the key from the back of a cupboard drawer, and unlocked and threw open the door to the girls' room.

"Did you get us that food? I'm famished." Gabby massaged her stomach.

He chuckled. It made him happy to see his shy twin opening up to him a little. "Yes, I did. Come on out and eat."

He stepped out of the way and allowed them to pass, keeping an eye on Evangeline. That one he didn't trust. She'd probably try and attack him with her finger nails, gouge his already injured face. He exhaled. Just like her mother. Their relationship had been tumultuous, to put it mildly. No matter how she treated him, he never once laid a finger on Bethany. On the contrary, she was the violent one. Maybe it was good it didn't work out between them or he suspected his injuries would have long surpassed a black eye, broken nose, and impaled foot. He'd been the victim of girlfriend abuse but knew that no one would ever believe him, especially considering her petite size.

Gabby took a bite of her date square. "Yum. Thanks for stopping by Coral's. We love her desserts." She took a swig of coffee. "And her coffee is the best. But it's lukewarm. May I use the microwave to heat it up?"

Percy yawned as sleepiness descended over him like a cloud. Must be the combination of stress and extra pills. Coffee. He needed more coffee to stay awake and remain one step ahead of these two daughters of his. "Yes, sweetie, you may. But not her." He glared at Evangeline, who hadn't said a word since he'd come home. "Knowing you, you'll heat it to scalding and toss it at my face. You can drink yours tepid."

"Did I ask you for anything? I happen to like it lukewarm. It pains me that you don't trust me." Evangeline's sly smile reeked of trouble. "By the way, if you knew why Gabby suggested you stop by Coral's Café, you would be denying her the chance to heat her coffee too. Did you forget that Gabby was the one who nailed your foot?"

Percy's brow wrinkled as he remembered Gabby's attacking role and the wink which she tried desperately to cover up when she suggested he go to Coral's for food. His eyes shot from Evangeline to Gabby and back again. He took a mouthful of the date square and swiped at the crumbs that trickled down his chin. "What are you trying to tell me?"

Evangeline snickered as she squared her shoulders. "Coral is a former Homicide Detective from Toronto. She helped catch Triple L, our town's murderer a few months ago. She's a very smart woman. By now, she's probably got the entire Lighthouse Landing police force onto you."

Worry bolted through him, but he shoved it away. "Ha. You can only hope. What would make her ever suspect me?" Percy's smart-aleck remark contradicted the unease charging through him. Did this Coral lady suspect him? Is that why she followed him? No matter. He'd gotten away. But seriously, what would be the odds of her figuring out that he had kidnapped the Fillmore twins? "Hurry up and eat because I changed my mind. That stunt you pulled, sending me to this Coral-previous-homicide-detective-person, has banished your freedom to roam the house. Not only can I not trust you, I'm tired and need a nap." He tipped the last of his coffee up to his mouth and missed. The brew poured down his chin and onto his T-shirt. Man, he was feeling mighty odd. "You're right. Best coffee and square dates I've ever had." A dizziness swept over him and he staggered a few steps.

Why was Evangeline eyeing him oddly? The girls blurred in front of him and the room tipped on an angle. Drat! He'd done a foolish thing, downing those extra pills. It was all that Coral woman's fault. "Get up girls. Take the remainder of your room to your treats …" His voice slurred and his words wouldn't form. "I mean … " He reached into his pocket for the key and that's the last thing he remembered.

Jace perched on the edge of his seat in the sergeant's office as he talked on the phone. "Hey Serg, I need to update you. We've had a few breaks in the Fillmore case. I talked to the Port Hope Adoption Agency, and Percy Winkles is indeed the twins' biological father. And he'd been seeking information about the location of his girls a few months ago. With this latest information, I think we might very well have our man. Now to figure out where he's taken them." He paused briefly to catch his breath. "What do you think?"

The door to Kensington's office opened and the man himself entered, phone to his ear. His brow furrowed, Jace contemplated him oddly before ending the call. "What are you doing here, Serg? Don't mind if I say so but you look awful. You should be home in bed."

Kensington coughed into his sleeve. The cough was so deep, he sounded like a growling bear. "Don't tell my wife. She'll kill me. I'm itching to be a part of this. I've had a soft spot for those girls for years, ever since the age of sixteen when they began their roles as my little green helpers when I played Santa Claus. I couldn't stay home and do nothing. So, take a hike Kelly. You've done a great job." He brought his elbow to his face and coughed again. "I'm taking over my office and I want you out. No sense exposing yourself to my germs."

Jace strode past him into the hallway. "Don't have to tell me twice."

The desk phone in Kensington's office rang. "Don't go yet, Kelly." He picked up the receiver and his eyes widened. "That's wonderful. Can you give me the number of the incoming call?" He reached for a pen and scribbled on a paper in front of him. "Thanks, Ed. Best news we've had all day. Don't give up hope that those girls of yours will be home soon. We'll keep in touch." He hung up the phone, his eyes as bright as his red nose. "That was Ed Fillmore. He just received a frantic call from Evangeline. It was short and he could barely hear her, but he thought she said something about them being in a swamp." The serg handed him the paper where he'd scribbled the number. "Ed's cell number is there too. Get Miller to help you with this. She'll need to use the triangulation software to see if she can figure out exactly where Evangeline's call was coming from. The only swamp around here is Thornton's Swamp, which is about a half hour drive from town." He rubbed his chin. "But it's vast. If he's holed up in there with them, it'll be quite the challenge to find them without that cell location."

"At least we know they're alive and have a general location of where they might be." Hope filled Jace. He didn't realize how much cases affected him until his chest felt a little bit lighter. Then he marvelled at Coral's insight. She really would make a valuable addition to the Lighthouse Landing force. He couldn't wait to tell her how bang on her hunch about Agitated Man was.

Angst filled him as he searched the building for Officer Andrea Miller. She was the last person he wanted to work with today. But he'd set aside his apprehension, be professional, and accept her expertise at tracing calls. Unable to locate her, he checked with Brittany at the main desk. "Do you know where Officer Miller might be?"

Brittany scowled. She pointed through the lobby to the parking lot, shook her head, and returned to studying the computer screen in front of her. Jace hurried through the lobby and stopped at the door. Miller leaned against the hood of Degroot's patrol car, smiling up at Luke. Degroot was smiling back. Hmmm. He didn't even realize Luke had returned from searching county roads for their suspect. He gritted his teeth. Luke wasn't his problem now as Kensington was behind his desk again. He opened the door and yelled out. "Finished already, Degroot?"

"No sign of him, sir."

"Okay, well, the sergeant is here. Maybe you should report that to him." He crooked a finger at the flirty female cop. "Miller, you're needed inside. Not my orders, believe me."

She whispered something in Luke's ear before heading toward the building. Luke chuckled. Jace frowned. He didn't like the looks of what seemed to be simmering between the two of them. Not that he'd say anything to Coral about it. If he did, it would appear that Jace was trying to discredit his opponent.

"What's going on?" Miller asked as she stepped past him into the station.

"Good news. Evangeline made a call to her father—something about being held in a swamp. Can you trace where the call was coming from?"

Her eyes lit up. "That's wonderful news and right up my alley. All I need are the phone numbers and I'm on it."

Jace handed her the paper then followed Miller's exaggerated hip-sway along the hallway. It was so pronounced he was surprised she didn't hip-check Officer Newton into the wall as he passed them from the other direction. Good grief. Was that her normal gait? Or was it dramatically altered for his benefit? She needn't waste her energy. At this rate, she'd need hip replacement surgery by the age of fifty. He coughed to conceal his laugh at the amusing thought, then choked on the obnoxious smell of her perfume. Strong scents on the job were not tolerated where he had previously worked. As soon as he took over as sergeant, he'd enforce that rule. Nowadays, many people were sensitive to strong scents, and it was only considerate to think of how others may react. To be honest, the smell reminded him of decaying Easter lilies. He much preferred the light fruity scent Coral wore.

He couldn't go there. It hurt too much. Instead he'd concentrate on catching Percy Winkles and bringing the Fillmore Twins home. An urgent excitement charged through him. He sensed they were on the cusp of catching Mr. Percy Winkles and returning the Fillmore twins to their loving parents. If only it was Coral at his side, helping apprehend the kidnapper. He missed her. A lot.

CHAPTER 20

Super Technology

A pounding inside Percy's skull throbbed worse than the time he had an abscessed tooth. Pressing both hands to the sides of his head, he groaned. He tried to roll over, but his right hip pained. What was wrong with him? He was falling apart at the young age of forty. His body trembled. Why was he so cold?

Forcing his eyes open, it took him a few seconds to focus through the haze. Why was he staring at his Jeep, Betsy, through the wide open front door? No wonder he was cold. Was he lying on the kitchen floor? *No! No!* Awareness dawned, and he shot to his feet.

My girls. Where are my girls? In a blurry stupor, Percy tripped over his own two feet as he scrambled toward the twins' room. He cursed when he spotted the door wide open. "Evangeline? Gabby?" He yelled frantically at the top of his lungs. When silence greeted him, he dropped to his knees, cradling his aching skull. They were gone. No. He couldn't lose them now—not after all those years of searching. "Now I know you hate me, God. You took my girls away from me not once but twice." His mournful wails echoed off the walls, rebounding with a merciless vengeance.

Not if I can help it!

Resolve bolted through him and he clambered to his feet. Stumbling toward the kitchen, he spied his cell phone on the kitchen counter. Odd. If they ran off, why wouldn't they take his phone to call for help? A new worry charged through him. Maybe they had already placed that call.

He pushed the button, but the screen was black. Great. The battery was dead. He must have forgotten to charge it last night. That's why they'd left it behind. Maybe fate was on his side after all and they hadn't been able to reach the authorities.

Still tipsy, he shuffled toward the open door and scanned the woods. It was unusually dark for midafternoon, and a light crackling sound met his ears. Freezing rain splattered off Betsy and coated the trees. Why hadn't the girls taken his truck? He checked his pockets for keys. Not there. What had he done with them? He charged through the place, searching in every hiding spot he'd ever used. Nothing. No wonder the girls couldn't steal the truck. In his drug-filled stupor he must have put them in an odd place. In a way, that worked to his advantage as the twins couldn't drive off. Of course, it meant he couldn't use his truck either until he located the keys. *Calm down, Percy. No need to fret. They won't get far in this weather.*

Percy reached under the kitchen sink and pulled out his hunting rifle. He hoped he wouldn't have to use it, but he'd bring it anyway, in case someone got in the way of getting his prized possessions back.

Slipping into his dark green rubber boots, camouflage hunting jacket, and woollen cap, he clutched the rifle, stepped outside, and closed the door. Those little elves of his couldn't have gotten very far, could they? How long had he been passed out? That was the question. As he strode past old Betsy, he glanced inside. His keys sat on the console. He tried the doors, and they were locked. Great! Those extra meds had really messed him up. And it was all that Coral woman's fault. Wait until he got his hands on her. Oh well, maybe it was all for the best. At least his daughters hadn't been able to escape via his Jeep. There was still a chance he could find them and get them back before the authorities were the wiser.

Percy clomped down the service road, studying the mud and melting snow. Years of hunting in the bush, mostly to survive when he didn't have an income, had honed his tracking skills. It didn't take him long to find two sets of small boot-prints with sharp, pointed heels. Locating the twins should be a piece of cake, especially with their green elf costumes—as long as he had light on his side. He cackled aloud. "Daddy's coming for you, girls. Daddy's coming."

The news channel predicted nasty weather, but she had to try. Coral turned the placard to *Closed*, locked her café, and hurried toward her car.

Earlier, while she'd been cleaning up the kitchen after a failed attempt to follow the alleged suspect, the vital information had popped into her brain. How could she have forgotten that Percy Winkles had slipped and mentioned a location when he was in McDonalds? Was the concussion wreaking havoc with her memory again?

The agitated man had declined the manager's free offer of ice-cream for his girls because he wouldn't get home before the cones melted. He'd started to mention where he lived then caught himself after saying the word *Thornton's*. When Coral searched for any surrounding streets or communities with that name, she came up blank. All except for one place—Thornton's Swamp. It not only existed but it was enormous. Coral sighed. If only she'd remembered this information earlier. She hoped it wasn't too late.

Bundling in her warmest clothes and boots, she climbed into her Elantra and drove toward the swamp. Coral made a right hand turn on Concession 7, taking the path she figured Percy Winkles might have driven, since it went right past the Fillmore Chicken Farm. Freezing rain splatted her windshield a short distance down the road. Great! She didn't even have snow tires on yet. How long could she possibly last in this weather without ditch-diving herself?

Trepidation settled in at her ludicrous quest. What in the world was she doing? Heading out alone, in horrible weather, to search a twenty-thousand-acre swamp? No weapon or backup? A niggle of foolishness settled over her. Perhaps she should let someone know where she was going.

Definitely not Luke. He'd tell her to stay out of police matters and remain in the kitchen. Her eyes swam as she recalled his harsh words. She swiped at a tear that trailed down her cheek. Sucking in a breath, she sniffled and forced herself to think of her mission. She'd deal with Luke later.

Jace, on the other hand, hadn't been distant, yet things were not the same between them. At least he'd listened to her abduction theory about the man possibly responsible for the twins' disappearance. A tightness in her chest made it hard to breathe as she also recalled Jace telling her to choose between him and Luke. Should she tell Jace of her mission right now? No. He'd also discourage her from going. She had to see if she could save the girls, although she didn't understand the desperate need that drove her. Did she miss police work that badly? Was the bakery not enough for her? Coral's shoulders slumped. So many questions but absolutely no answers.

As she reached the end of Concession 7, she tapped her thumbs on the steering wheel as she debated. Should she turn left or right on County Road 1? She knew from studying the map that either way would take a person in the direction of the swamp. Hmmm. A sign for Thornton's Swamp Camping urged her left. Okay, she'd follow it. It made the most sense to her, although she didn't really know why.

Freezing rain fell thickly now, and her windshield wipers could barely keep up. Coral chastised herself. Her mission was insane. She knew it in her head, but not in her heart.

God, give me wisdom and protection and help me find the girls.

She hoped that, since Percy Winkles had driven into Lighthouse Landing the last few days, he was hiding the women on the western end of the swamp, where the campground was. Maybe he was holed up in a building of some sort, possibly a yurt since it was winter. She couldn't imagine they'd be outdoors. Didn't most campgrounds have buildings such as stores, supply sheds, park offices, and visitor centres?

A large blue sign with an arrow pointing right advertised camping again at the next side-road. Twenty-six kilometres ahead? Her stomach sank. Should she take it? Why not? This place was as good as any to start looking.

Jace clenched his clammy hands as he paced behind Miller. She was employing the software to trace Evangeline's call. When the signal pinged off a nearby cell tower, revealing the location, Jace felt like yelling out a loud *Whoop*! But he restrained himself to a low-key "Bingo". Technology today was really amazing. Although he knew this software existed, he'd never personally used it while in TO.

His elation was short-lived when Miller explained the area to him. Thornton's Swamp was twenty thousand acres in size. Could that be right? Jace scratched the back of his head. How in the world could the guy survive in the winter in the middle of a swamp? And why would he take the women there?

"The swamp is vast, and the location is not exact. It pinged in the southwest corner." Miller pointed to the spot on her screen. "As far as I can tell, it's in the campground area."

"Thanks, Miller, I'm going to get this information to Kensington pronto." Jace sped-walked down the hallway and almost ran into Luke carrying a mug of coffee as he exited the lunchroom. "There's been a break in the case. I'd fill you in but I'm in a hurry. I'm sure Miller would be delighted to inform you." Jace let the remark slip then chastised himself for being unprofessional.

Jace sprinted through the lobby and down the hallway to Kensington's office. Hand on the doorknob, he peered in the glass window at the top and froze. Drat! Serg was on the phone. He'd have to wait. Judging by the sheepish look on Kensington's face, the wife must have tracked him down. Jace let go of the knob, shoved his hands in his pockets, and shifted from one foot to the other. Getting a search going quickly was of the outmost importance. As he debated whether to barge into the man's office, Kensington waved him in and hung up the phone. Jace opened the door so quickly it crashed against the wall. "Sorry about that." He hurried to his boss's desk and thumped a fist on it. "We've got a possible location where the twins are being held."

The sergeant jumped and held up his hands toward Jace. "Whoa there, Kelly. Calm down. Where are they?"

Embarrassment fell over Jace. "I apologize, sir. Sometimes I get a little over-exuberant, but I'm raring to go. It's Thornton's Swamp."

"Really. That's great news." Kensington tugged a tissue from the box on his desk, tipped his head back, and sneezed. "Excuse me. I'd go into the hallway if I were you." Kensington swiped at his flaming crimson nose. Jace reversed until he was standing in the doorway. Due to the pressing emergency, he'd temporarily forgotten that the sergeant was sick.

Kensington blew his nose; the sound reminded Jace of a boat horn's blast. "That place is enormous. Finding them might be darn near impossible."

"The triangulation software gave a generalized location, and it appears it may be in the campground."

Kensington sniffled. "Good. That narrows it down a little. Take Degroot with you. If you run into the kidnapper, you'll need additional brawn. I'm heading home to bed. Not only did the wife track me down, but I fear I did a stupid thing coming in. I hope and pray that I haven't spread this around." Kensington shooed him farther away with a wave of his hand. "Steer way clear of my office if you know what's good for you." He reached for a spray bottle of disinfectant and wiped his phone and the arm rests of his chair. "Please keep me apprised of any news."

Jace took a step to leave, but Kensington's voice stopped him. "Oh, and a few other things. We're under a freezing rain warning, so be careful on the roads. You only have a few hours of daylight left, meaning you may not be able to complete much of your search today. Also, this may not be anything, but Sylvia went by Coral's to pick up *something* and the place was closed. She really wanted that *something*, which I believe is an anniversary cake, so you may want to check on Coral and make sure she's okay. I know she's really struggled with her health, particularly her memory, since that concussion at the hands of our dastardly coroner. It's probably nothing and she simply forgot about the cake."

Worry charged through Jace. When was the last time he'd talked to Coral? Wasn't it this afternoon when she tried to follow the man she suspected of kidnapping the twins? Had the suspect come back and threatened her? Or worse yet, harmed her? A sick feeling settled in the pit of his stomach as he hurried down the hall to find Degroot. Of course, Big Dutch was with Miller, leaning over her shoulder staring at the map of the swamp.

"Degroot. We're heading to Thornton's Swamp."

"Yeah, yeah. I hear you." He flapped a hand over his shoulder.

"You and me. Now," Jace barked.

Luke shot up as if a bolt of lightning had struck him. "Right." His voice was compliant, but his eyes threw daggers.

CHAPTER 21

Man Talk and Freezing Rain

As the officers left the station parking lot, Jace noticed Coral's *Closed* sign in her café window. Maybe she truly *was* having a bad day with her health and decided to take a nap. Was it anything more serious than that? Had Percy Winkles returned to take care of his perceived threat, sensing that Coral was on to him? Jace wished he had time to follow up on her to make sure she was okay. He glanced at Luke who was carefully navigating the slippery roads. "The sergeant mentioned that his wife, Sylvia, stopped by Coral's bakery to pick up an order and it was all closed up. You wouldn't know if Coral had an appointment or something, would you?"

"Nope. Haven't talked to Coral since last evening." Luke's response was gruff and to the point as he stared out the windshield.

Jace studied the man. He couldn't figure him out. Luke was different lately. Not his usual positive self. Jace tapped in a call to Coral's cell. It rang until it went to voice mail. Concern dropped over him like a weighted blanket. It was the middle of the day. Where would she be? Was she in that dead of a sleep that she didn't hear her phone? Of course, she could have set it to silent mode if she didn't want to be disturbed.

"Can't get her?" Luke hurled a hooded glance his way. "Perhaps she's lying down with a migraine again. She's suffered continually from those since her concussion, but then, you wouldn't know that since you weren't around." A muscle in his jaw twitched. "I've been there for her every day, checking on her health, clearing snow from her parking lot and driveway, and unloading deliveries. I've always treated her like a queen, yet she's kept me at arm's length. You can have her. I'm done trying. What good is a love that's one-sided?"

Jace wrestled with conflicting emotions—guilt over his absence when Coral was sick and elation over the fact that Luke had given up. Jace shifted in his seat. "I'm going to be honest with you, Luke. I'm not so sure it's one-sided. Believe it nor not, I had my reasons for staying silent these last several weeks, but I don't wish to go into them right now." Jace grasped Luke's shoulder, which was sagging with despondent resignation. "Thank you for taking care of Coral. You're right. I should have checked up on her, but I didn't want to get in the way."

"What do you mean?" Deep furrow lines etched Luke's forehead.

Jace wet his lips. He couldn't believe he was going to let it all out—and to his adversary for Coral's heart. "Even before I walked in on that kiss in the hospital room, I felt there was something between you and Coral. As much as it pains me to say this, I didn't want to interfere if you were the man she was meant to be with. I still don't want to get in the way. From everything I've witnessed, you are a good man, and I've no doubt you would make Coral happy."

The trench lines in Luke's brow gave way to one raised eyebrow. "You thought Coral had feelings for me?"

"Yes. In fact, I know she did. Probably still does. Did you know I was going to propose that day? I had an engagement ring in the giftbag."

Luke gripped the steering wheel tightly as he skidded to a stop at the end of Concession 7. "What? You were going to ask Coral to marry you?"

Jace pointed at the campground sign. "I think we should make a left here, Degroot."

Luke nodded as he made his turn.

"Yes, but I fell into a downward tailspin after witnessing that kiss between the two of you. So, coward that I am, I dropped the ring and ran. Never did propose. Told her she had to decide between us."

Luke shook his head. "I didn't know any of that. Coral never told me about the ring. If I had known, I would have stepped back. I'm really sorry. I was losing my dad that day and Coral had been a rock—a sympathetic ear—throughout that terribly emotional time." His voice wavered. "I couldn't lose her too."

For a moment, the only sound was the thump-thump-thumping of the wipers against the windshield and the crackle of rain as it hit the car.

Jace's heart softened toward Big Dutch. Despite the issues with his own father, Jace still had him. After this case was over, he'd try harder at restoring the relationship between them. "No. I didn't want you to step back. Still don't. My silence these last few months was to give Coral time to decide between the two of us. As a man of faith, I prayed diligently. I've prepared myself, as much as possible, for the possibility that she might choose you. But this waiting phase is killing me."

"Tell me about it." Luke pursed his lips, his features drawn and pale.

"In fact, I told her to hurry up, because if you're the lucky candidate, I'm declining the job in Lighthouse Landing. It would be too painful for me to be in town."

"I hear you."

"There's another sign for the campground." Jace pointed. "It's twenty-six kilometres yet. I hope we're on the right track."

Luke nodded. "Me too."

"You can tell me it's none of my business, but what's going on with you and Miller?"

Degroot rubbed the back of his neck. "I don't know. It's complicated. Before Coral came to Lighthouse Landing, Andrea and I had gone out a few times. I really thought we had something special until I discovered she was sneaking around behind my back with the mayor." Luke twisted his neck back and forth until it cracked. "Sorry, I must have slept funny. Got a kink in my neck. Anyway, I confronted her, then promptly broke it off. It hurt, but I got over it. I figured it was all for the best since we were coworkers, and a relationship wouldn't be appropriate. Her fling with Mayor Manicotti ended up on the rocks after the mayor started his own clandestine affair with Officer Victoria Woods. Ironic, isn't it? The mayor did to her what she did to me. I guess that Bible verse rings true—do unto others what you would have them do to you."

The patrol car fishtailed a little on the icy roads. Luke quickly let go of his neck, eased off the gas, and gripped the wheel tightly with both hands. "Andrea's been off on sick leave for the last six months and only recently returned. She wants to pick up from where we left off, but I'm not so sure."

Jace bit his bottom lip. Should he give Big Dutch advice? It wasn't as though Jace had enough experience with women to offer his opinion. But he figured he knew what he'd do in such a situation. "You can take or leave my suggestion, but I wouldn't trust a woman who was deceptively involved with another man on the side."

Luke tilted his head in his direction. "You puzzle me. Why wouldn't you be pushing me towards Miller? That way, Coral's attention would be all yours. You know, I'm glad we had this talk. I had a skewed impression of you from the start. I think we got off on the wrong foot." Eyes still on the road, he delivered a playful punch to Jace's shoulder. "May the best man win."

Jace chuckled. "You're on, Big Dutch."

Darkness was closing in and it was only four o'clock. Of course, the low-lying, ashen clouds and shadowed woods on either side of the heavily-forested road didn't help. The rain was continual— Coral's windshield wipers could barely keep up. What was she doing? Perhaps the concussion had addlepated her common sense. She chewed her bottom lip. Would this road ever end? Where was that campground? As frustration mounted, a sign appeared in the distance. She squinted to read it. Phew. Only one more kilometre. The paved road shimmered in front of her, and she eased her foot off the accelerator a bit more. It was nothing short of a miracle that her car had stayed on the icy roads this long.

Ahead, a small kiosk emerged. Must be the campground registration office. As she approached, she could see that the blinds in the building were shut and an orange gate arm was broken off partway—one jagged section lying on the ground. Had someone desperately wanted to camp? Was that someone Percy Winkles?

She followed a notice for camping and yurts. Within a few minutes, she'd circled every loop available. No sign of life or the Jeep Wagoneer. Then an arrow announced Thornton's Visitor Centre two kilometres ahead. May as well check that out while she was here.

She'd only driven a short distance when her car angled sideways, slipped off onto the shoulder of the road, and wedged itself in mud. Great. Coral tried driving forward, then back, but the more she tried, the deeper she sank and the farther she tipped toward the ditch.

Ice crystals stung her face as she climbed from the car to assess the dicey dilemma. She pulled the hood of the parka over her head and glided on boots across the glassy road to the rear of her Elantra. Both back tires were buried in mud to the tops of their hubcaps. *Great!* There was absolutely no way she was getting out of here anytime soon. Foolish woman. Not only had she spent the last forty-five minutes searching in vain, she was now hopelessly stuck.

She'd have to swallow her pride and call for help. Hopefully the automobile club would find her quickly and neither Luke nor Jace would ever have to know about her insane trek into an enormous swamp, in the middle of an ice-storm, to apprehend a kidnapper. Oh boy. When she put it all together like that, her mission came off as foolhardy at best.

Fishing her cell from her pocket, her shoulders sagged when she realized that she'd missed several calls from Jace. Bummer. It had been on silent mode. Maybe that was a good thing. Jace would have insisted she halt her extremely reckless mission immediately, that is, if he had been able to get the information out of her. Not that she would have lied to the man, but critical details may not have been forthcoming. Rolling her eyes at the devious thought, she ducked inside the car and returned his call. *Every inclination of a man's heart is sinful from birth*. How truly personal that Scripture was to her at the moment.

"Kelly."

"Jace? It's me."

"Coral? I've been worried about you. Kensington is concerned too. His wife Sylvia stopped by to get some baking she'd ordered, and you were closed."

Coral gasped, her fingers touching her lips. "Oh no. I totally forgot she was picking up the cake today. I'll call her. Hopefully she'll understand."

"What will she understand? Are you ill?"

"No ... I ... did a dumb thing." She chewed on a fingernail. "Please don't be angry with me."

"Why am I not surprised? What did you do?"

"I'm stuck in the mud in the campground in Thornton's Swamp."

"What in the world are you doing there? How did you know?"

Coral bit her fingernail a little too ardently, nipping the flesh. She flinched. "So I was right about Percy Winkles hiding the twins here?"

"We think so. The main thing is that we find you before our suspect does. Luke and I are only a few minutes away. Stay put. Where exactly are you?"

"I'm ..."

A gush of cold air blew into the vehicle as her driver's door flew open. A quick turn of her head and she found herself staring directly into the barrel of a rifle.

"Hang up now," the man ordered gruffly.

Coral's mouth went completely dry. She held up a palm toward him. "Okay, Percy, don't shoot. I'm hanging up." She tapped the phone icon with her thumb, tossed the device on the passenger seat, and raised both hands. "Done."

"Get out of your car."

Heart pounding wildly in her chest, Coral slowly slid from her seat and stood face to face with the kidnapper. She took a moment to study him. Rain dripped off the edge of his flattened, cockeyed nose. One eye was ringed in morose ugly purple, accentuating his wild and desperate look.

"You are nothing but a pain in my backside. You're coming with me." He nudged her forward with the tip of his weapon.

"Where are we going? Where are the twins?"

"Shut up. You talk too much."

"Sorry."

"Walk about six feet ahead of me and stay there so I can keep an eye on you."

Stinging rain fell even heavier now, and Coral struggled to stay upright, slipping several times on the ice. At one point, she slid toward the ditch running alongside the road, but after performing some sort of funky dance, she managed to avoid a fall. Shivers skittered through her, although she wasn't sure if they were from the evil man behind her or the weather. Probably a horrifying combo.

"Those darn girls got away on me and it's all your fault," Percy grumbled.

The girls had gotten away? Hope galloped through Coral. She tried to keep the excitement from her voice. "My fault? I wasn't even here. How can you blame me?"

"If you hadn't followed me after I left your bakery, I wouldn't have stressed, swallowed extra pills, and passed out. That's when those smart girls took advantage of me and escaped. When Evangeline mentioned you had previously been a homicide detective, I figured you were on to me. Unfortunately, my plan to take the twins and run didn't happen because of you. As a result of your meddlesome interference, I've lost my daughters." He snarled. "I ought to drop you right now."

Yay! The twins had gotten away. Her elation was zapped by the man's deadly threat. Would he follow through on his dire warning? Could her life be over in an instant? Fear and confusion hung over her, heavier than the oppressive weather system. "Did I hear you correctly? Did you call the girls your daughters?"

"Yes, they're biologically mine. They were put up for adoption as babies against my wishes. Bethany and I were teenagers and not ready to be parents, but I was willing to try. I'd been searching for them my whole life when I found them right here in Lighthouse Landing. No one, and I mean absolutely no one, is going to take them from me now. It's imperative that I get them back." His words were edged in hysteria.

Coral's mind raced. She hadn't heard that the twins were adopted, but then she was fairly new to the area. Was it possible? Or was this man living in a delusional world? A strong impulse came over her to play the sympathy card. Pausing on the road, she turned toward him. "I'm so sorry to hear that, Percy. It must have been absolutely heart-wrenching to go through what you did. If that were my situation, I'd want to keep my daughters too."

The kidnapper's eyes narrowed. "How did you know?"

Coral tilted her head. "Know what?"

"How did you know I had the Fillmore twins? More importantly, how did you know where to find us?"

Coral shrugged. "I've been praying for the safety of those women—asking God to reveal what lies in darkness. I believe he told me."

"Darkness? What are you talking about?" His words were shaky. "God told you? Ha! With talk like that, I can understand how you got demoted from your position in homicide to bakery chef." He circled a finger at his temple.

"Mock if you will, but you really don't know what you're talking about it. I didn't hear God audibly. He spoke to me in here." She pointed at her chest. "I had reservations about you from the moment I saw you. I believe God placed those hints in my heart because I prayed that the kidnapper's sins would be found out and the girls kept safe."

Percy's complexion paled as fear flickered in his irises. "What?" His eyes darted heavenward. "I can't believe it. Pastor Elliott warned me. He told me God was after me. That prison chaplain told me God loved me, but I find that hard to believe. No one has ever loved me." His voice cracked. "Don't you get it? That's why I want my daughters. I'm sure I can convince them to love me."

Coral's heart softened a little. "I'm sure they would love you if they got to know you. Why don't we end this right now before your kidnapping charge escalates to murder? I'll advocate in the courts for a lesser sentence."

"You'd do that for me?"

"Yes, I would."

Don't make promises that you are unsure you can keep. Her inner voice convicted her, but … wasn't placating the man top priority at the moment? "As I see it, you have a choice to make. Let the girls go back to the only home they've ever known, or possibly spend the rest of your life rotting in prison on kidnapping charges."

Percy's expression twisted with torment. His chest rose and fell rapidly, his eyes flashing—soft one moment then rage-filled the next. Suddenly he spat on the road. "I've no compassion. The Fillmores had them for twenty-two years, and now it's my turn." He waved the gun around in the air. "You're wasting precious time—time I could be using to find my girls. They've been out in the elements for a while now. Get going."

As soon as she turned, the gun jammed her hard in the back. The force sent her teetering off-balance. Her arms wind-milled wildly through the air in a desperate attempt to stay upright. She lost the battle, landing hard on her bottom on the icy road, the wind knocked out of her. She gasped at the pain that radiated across her tailbone. Not again. That area hadn't completely healed from her tumble down the steps last week. Moaning, she rolled onto her right side and curled into a ball on the frozen surface.

Percy boot-skated the few steps until he was at her side. Yanking her by the arm, he hauled her to her feet. Coral moaned again. The combination of pain, swift position change, and ongoing health issues with her concussion made her world spin terribly. "Quit being so dramatic and get going. It's almost dark."

Blinking away the dizziness, she gritted her teeth against the waves of pain shooting through her lower back. Her ire rose. Percy had made a grave mistake. A determined resolve to beat this dude ignited inside. No more mild-mannered pastry chef. Hello fiery homicide detective. "Stop pushing me and I may be able to stay on my feet." Coral hissed the words at him.

"You got yourself in this predicament by following me. All of this is of your own doing."

Despite the fact that he made a valid point, her mind swirled with plans for the outrageous charade forming in her mind. If he thought the reaction to her fall was dramatic, wait until he experienced the opening lines of what would make a blockbuster movie, *Ditch the Kidnapper*. Coral stared past him into the bush, her eyes widening. "Run girls, run! He's got a gun."

Percy spun, searching the forest behind him. Seizing her opportunity, she ran at him, shoving him with all the force she could muster. His gun went airborne as his arms and legs flew in all directions. His rifle disappeared with him as he toppled headfirst into the muddy ravine. Frantic to escape, Coral whirled and broke into a half-run, half-slide on the slippery surface, biting back the pain in her tailbone. If she couldn't find a way into the woods, she'd be an easy target once he climbed from the ditch.

"You witch," Percy yelled from somewhere behind her.

Coral stumbled down the mucky embankment on the opposite side of the road and crashed into the dark woods. Charging through the bush, she grimaced against searing buttock pain and branches smacking across her face. A shot rang out, the bullet splintering a tree nearby. Yikes. Coral ducked, her breaths coming fast and heavy. She had to get deeper. Pushing hard, she crashed through the trees until she couldn't run anymore.

Bent over, hands on knees, she gasped for oxygen as she listened for sounds that the dangerous man approached. But she heard no snapping of branches, only the crackling of rain against the trees. Where did she go from here?

Slowly she straightened. Coral relaxed a little as the pain in her backside diminished. Perhaps the fall hadn't caused as much damage as she'd first thought. She strained to see as twilight settled in. How would she ever help the girls now? She was lost in the woods and had absolutely no idea where to look for them. Would she freeze to death? Suffer a fatal bullet wound? A strange green light glowed in the distance, and for some reason, she headed toward it.

The faces of Jace Kelly and Luke Degroot flashed before her. Would they be able to find her now? Could she survive long enough to inform them of the decision her heart had finally made? Because somewhere in the middle of all this chaos, the answer rang loud and clear.

CHAPTER 22

Bizarre Legends and Green Lights

Don't shoot. Her words haunted him. "Coral?" Jace screamed into the phone although deep inside he knew it was futile. The call had ended suddenly, and fear for her safety tightened around him like a boa constrictor's death-squeeze.

Luke grabbed his arm. "What's wrong?"

"Percy's got her." Jace's heart beat so erratically he thought he might be sick. "And he threatened to shoot her."

"What? I warned her to stay out of things. Why didn't she listen?" Luke slapped the dashboard. "That darn woman. She's too stubborn for her own good."

"Somehow Coral discovered where our kidnapper was holed up with the Fillmore twins, went out on her own search, slipped off the road, and got stuck in the mud near the campground. While she was talking to me, he found her."

"At least we're not far away." Luke clenched his jaw, his eyes darkening.

"No, but we need to get there fast." Jace studied Luke as the big officer pressed on the accelerator. The man seemed more angry than worried. Was this the way Big Dutch reacted when concerned? Jace wasn't angry at all—only beside himself with fear. He couldn't lose Coral. He just couldn't. It pained him to admit that, even if Coral chose Luke over him, Jace didn't want to see a hair on her beautiful head damaged. He loved her with every fibre of his being. He didn't know such a love was possible. *Please God, protect her, even if my love for her can never be fully realized.*

"There's her car." Luke pointed at the Elantra that was tipped on a funny angle toward the ditch. He pulled the cruiser parallel to her vehicle and stopped.

"I'll take a quick look around." Jace set one boot on the road and his leg slid out from underneath him. He grabbed the door for support. "It's a skating rink out here."

"No kidding. Glad Kensington had us get snow tires installed already. Be careful, Kelly."

Jace donned gloves, opened the Elantra door, and peered inside. Coral's cell phone was on the passenger seat and her purse lay on the floor mat below. Dread filled him. Where did Percy take her? He straightened and stared down the road as icy rain stung his face and neck. What a day! The weather was as bad as the horrific circumstances. He glided to the cruiser and ducked inside.

"Coral's cell and purse are in the car. Percy obviously has her. I don't see any signs of a …" his voice broke, "… struggle. Thank God."

"That's good news, at least. Where do we even begin to look?"

"Since no vehicle passed us while we were driving toward the campground, I think we should follow the road in and see where it leads, assuming our kidnapper hauled Coral off in his Jeep."

Luke's eyes darted in all directions as he peered through the windshield. "Agreed. I have to say this area gives me the creeps, even without the dangerous situation we're facing. I camped here as a boy and, although I never saw it, I believe it existed."

"Saw what?" Jace scanned the edge of the treeline as Luke drove forward.

"The green light."

"What are you talking about, Degroot?"

"The legend. A mysterious green light in the woods has been documented by people as far back as the mid eighteen-hundreds. Even hunters have been known to freak out and run when it appears."

Jace glanced at him, his eyebrows raised. "What? That's absurd. There must be a logical scientific explanation for that." He turned back to study the black, now rather spooky, line of trees.

Luke shrugged. "Just saying."

Not far ahead the paved road turned into a dirt road with a sign pointing to Thornton's Visitor Centre. "I remember coming to this place with my family. They had a cool owl exhibit."

The officers bounced in their seats along the rutted, muddy, pot-holed lane. After the road took a sharp turn, the headlamps illuminated a building in the distance. Parked in front was the infamous Jeep Wagoneer. "Bingo. We found them. Stop here, Degroot."

Luke killed the engine, along with the headlights.

Jace shoved the car door open with his shoulder. "Let's walk the rest of the way in. Hopefully we can use the element of surprise to catch him."

Weapons at the ready, both officers skirted the treeline on opposite sides of the road and approached the Visitor Centre. With a flick of his hand, Jace signalled for Luke to head around back while he handled the front. "Police, open up," Jace commanded. Silence. He waited a few seconds then kicked at the door, which gave way under the pressure and slammed against the inside wall. Weapon raised, he squinted into the darkness. Nothing moved inside. Jace felt for a switch and clicked it to light up the interior. He performed a quick search of the small building and radioed for Luke to come in. "Inside. All clear."

Luke joined him and together they did a more thorough search. The main door opened into a library with a soft pink fabric armchair and matching couch. Rows of books lined dark-stained wooden bookshelves. Stuffed birds and animals were perched along the upper edge of the shelves. A doorway to the right led down a hall where nature scenes were displayed along the walls. The first room on their left was a kitchen or lunchroom. A white pastry box sat on the counter.

"He was here all right." Luke glanced inside the box. "He obviously went to Coral's because those are her date squares. I'd recognize them anywhere. They're Kensington's favourite."

Across the hall was a tiny storage area with boxes and filing cabinets taking up almost the entire space. Next was a washroom. At the far end was a larger room with a mattress on the floor. "This must be where he kept the girls." Jace sighed. Hopefully he hadn't harmed them in any way. "So where are Percy, Coral, and the Fillmore Twins? Why is his vehicle still here?"

Luke rubbed his chin. "Since we didn't pass any cars on the way in, or anyone on foot, they must be in the woods somewhere."

"It seems the most likely scenario. Let's retreat to Coral's car and search from there." Jace headed for the door. "Maybe we can trace footprints in the mud or something."

"Makes the most sense."

When the officers reached the Jeep, Jace cupped his hands against the glass and peered inside. He tried the door. "Keys are on the console and the doors are locked." Hope sparked inside him and an anxious half-chuckle flew from his mouth. "It appears our kidnapper made a little mistake. That little mistake might save the women's lives."

Luke nodded. "God works in mysterious ways when we pray."

"You've got it, Big Dutch." Jace mulled over his comrade's latest remark. Luke had been praying? Was the angry façade the man had presented a few minutes ago on learning Coral's life was in jeopardy Luke's reaction to fear then, as Jace had wondered?

"Did you have a nickname in Toronto?" Luke asked as they clomped through the mud toward the cruiser.

"Sure did. Since it's not one I'm proud of, I'd rather not mention it." Jace slid onto the passenger seat and Luke started the engine.

Luke hurled him a half-grin as he did a three-point turn. "Guess I'll start calling you Sergeant Kelly then, because that's who you'll be to me soon."

Jace appreciated Luke's light-hearted attempt to defuse stress while both of them were terribly worried for Coral's life and the lives of the twins. As they jostled along the uneven terrain again, another possibility entered Jace's mind. Should he read more into Luke calling him by his future title? Did Luke assume Jace would win Coral's heart and stay in Lighthouse Landing? Didn't Luke say only a few miles back that he hoped the best man would win? No matter. Kelly shoved aside their personal dilemma and concentrated on the desperate situation they were in. Timing was critical, not only for the twins' lives but for Coral's.

Coral held her hands out in front of her face to feel her way along. Trekking through dense woods in the pitch black was impossibly dangerous. She couldn't count the times she tripped over rocks or tree roots and almost face-planted on the forest floor. Slowly and carefully she made her way toward the green glow. She had no idea what it was, but at least it was something to focus on. Was she heading straight into trouble?

Her original plan when she fled from the kidnapper was to stay parallel to the road so as not to get lost. At first, she could view it in the distance through the trees. Not any longer. She could only hope her internal compass would be true to her conscious desire.

A whooshing sound came at the same time as something whizzed past her face. She froze in her tracks. Had Percy Winkles found her? The flapping of wings put that fear to rest.

Heartrate charging, she wet her lips and took a step. A branch cracked loudly, and the green light disappeared. Odd. She waited, unsure of what to do. Had she alerted the dangerous man to her location? Was he at the other end of the green light? As far as she could discern, he should still be somewhere behind her.

When the green light appeared again, she made her way toward it—unable to rationally explain the draw. Only a few feet away now, she sensed a presence at her right side. A crushing pain slammed her hard across the shoulder before she had time to react. Reeling in agony, she slumped to her knees.

CHAPTER 23

Two-headed Aliens

Luke parked the cruiser facing Coral's Elantra. Jace climbed out and glanced heavenward. *God, help us find them.* Night had settled over the woods, but the freezing rain had changed to a light drizzle. Jace was reminded that there was always something to be thankful for.

"Don't you think we should end this search and resume in the morning? How much can we see with flashlights?" Luke folded his arms across his bulletproof vest and leaned against the patrol car.

"We're so close, I can feel it. Let's give it an hour. If we come up blank, we'll go."

Luke nodded. "Okay."

"Why don't we start by searching along the sides of the road for any clues as to where the kidnapper would have taken Coral." Jace pointed. "You take the south shoulder and I'll take the north."

Jace hadn't gone far when his beam of light picked up a colourful object. Excitement coursed through him. "Degroot?" He whispered across the road. "Found something."

When Luke joined him, Kelly lit up the lavender toque at the edge of the ditch. "Doesn't that belong to Coral?"

"I'm fairly certain it does. It looks similar to the one she wore the evening of the Christmas Parade." Luke toed the article of clothing lightly with his boot. "Judging by its condition, it hasn't been here long. It's got to be hers."

"Note the footprints climbing up the side of the ditch and heading into the woods. Let's go."

Jace didn't wait for Luke's reply but charged into the muddy ravine and scrambled up the slippery embankment. He heard Luke clambering around behind him as he entered the woods.

"It's pitch black in here. This is going to be a difficult search." Luke complained in his ear.

"We'll follow the snapped branches and crushed vegetation. Can you see them?" Jace scattered the beam of light around.

"Yes. Sort of. I'll let you lead." Luke fell in behind him.

On her knees, swaying from the pain that was still rippling across her right shoulder, Coral squinted into the oppressive blackness, trying to make sense of what had happened. Had Percy found her? If so, why hadn't he shot her instead of slamming her with a heavy object? Not that she was complaining about that.

"Coral?" A blinding brightness made her blink. "I'm so sorry. Let me help you. I didn't mean to hit you. I thought you were that horrible Percy and he'd found us." A young woman clasped her arm and helped her to her feet.

"Evangeline?" Coral blinked rapidly in an attempt to clear her vision.

"I'm Gabby. She's Evangeline." Gabby pointed toward her sister who was sitting on a pile of leaves, her back against a large rock, flashlight in hand. "How did you find us?"

"By following the green glow."

Gabby dropped the large branch and it hit the ground with a thump. "I told you it would still be visible, Evangeline. Covering the flashlight with your elf-hat didn't help much."

"It was a smart idea." Coral massaged her aching shoulder. "I wouldn't have found you without it. But Percy is out there looking for me, for all of us, so we'll have to use the light sparingly or we'll draw him to us. And he has a rifle. He shot at me, so I don't need to underscore how dangerous he is."

"He told us he'd never hurt us, but I knew we couldn't believe him. What do we do now? I'm afraid." Evangeline shivered as she aimed the light at the ground.

An idea formed in Coral's brain. "My car is back there on the road. If we can find it, we can get away." That fact that it was stuck in the mud seemed a minor complication at the moment.

"That's a great idea except Evangeline is hurt. She twisted her ankle badly while we were running in the dark. I think it's broken." Gabby moved to her sister's side.

Coral dropped to a knee. "Shine your light here for a minute, Evangeline." Coral tenderly prodded around the swollen joint. "I don't think it's broken, but I can't say for sure. Can you put any weight on it?"

"I don't know. I'll try."

Coral held one arm while Gabby took the other. Together they helped Evangeline to her feet. One step and she cried out in pain.

"I guess not. Okay, I'll piggyback you. Being tall has its advantages and you can't weigh very much. Hop on." Coral turned her back to the twin.

Evangeline giggled. "I haven't had one of those in years. Can you help me up, Gabby?"

Grimacing against shoulder and coccyx pain, Coral grabbed the featherweight twin behind the knees to secure her position. The added weight would surely stress her injuries, but necessity warranted it. "We'll need the flashlight to find our way, Evangeline. Cover it with your hat again and aim it at the forest floor as much as possible so as not to draw attention."

Coral whispered a quick prayer that she was moving in the right direction. While Evangeline flickered the light over Coral's shoulder, Coral searched for evidence of her previous steps. Gabby flanked them, carrying the large branch.

"Thank you for finding us," Evangeline whispered in Coral's ear.

"You're welcome. Now, let's get you both safely home."

"There's a bullet lodged in that tree." Jace's light exposed a splintered and damaged trunk. "It definitely looks fresh. The suspect must have gotten a shot off at Coral, or perhaps the twins."

"This is absolutely crazy," Luke grumbled as they shoved branches out of the way and sidestepped rocks. "Don't get me wrong. I want to find Coral and the Fillmore Twins as much as you do, but seriously? What can we accomplish in this intense darkness?"

"Under any other circumstances I'd agree. But we're so close … only minutes behind Coral and her abductee. Let's try a little longer. If you want to give up, go ahead and leave, but I'm continuing."

Luke sighed. "Don't be ridiculous. I'm not going to abandon my partner." He skidded to a halt as a chunk of ice fell from an overhead branch and crashed onto his head.

"What's wrong? Did you hear something?" Jace whispered.

"You mean, besides the ice that was walloping me on the head?" Luke brushed shards off his hat and jacket. "Yes. I saw that green light—the one I told you about. Directly ahead and coming right at us." His voice shook. "Turn off your flashlight, Kelly."

Jace complied with his colleague's request, and the pair of officers stood in the pitch black. "Seriously, Degroot? I don't see anything. You're letting a legend from a century ago dilute your common sense. Or did that falling ice cause damage to your brain?"

"I'm not so sure it's a legend. I actually know of a hunter who reported seeing it only a few years ago." He clasped Jace's shoulder. "Look! It's getting closer. Can't you see it?"

Jace strained to see but came up blank. "I don't see anything, but listen."

Crunching leaves and snapping twigs signalled someone or something's approach. Jace pulled Degroot behind a stand of trees with him. "It could be our guy."

Luke spoke softly near Jace's ear. "The green light is getting closer, and I see two beings. One appears human and the other has extra appendages extending from its sides." Luke's voice grew louder. "And it has two heads."

"Zip it, Degroot. You're going to give our position away. When they, or it, gets closer, blind it with your flashlight." He waited a few seconds. "Now."

A scream sliced the air the second Luke's light exposed three sets of wide, white eyeballs. When Jace saw a little green elf and a tall woman with another elf on her back, relief weakened his knees so much he nearly crumpled to the ground. His eyes locked onto Coral's. "We found you. Thank God." He nudged Degroot with an elbow. "And we're so relieved you're not little green aliens. Let's get out of here."

CHAPTER 24

A Light Extinguished

Little green aliens? What was that supposed to mean? Coral shrugged. Jace and Luke stood in front of her. Nothing else mattered at the moment. "How did you find us?"

Jace cleared his throat and tossed a sideways grin at Luke. "We saw, rather Luke saw, your green light approaching. I heard you."

The two men exchanged glances. Jace's face held amusement while Luke's cheeks flushed in the warm glow of Evangeline's flashlight. Whatever was that about? No matter. Coral sighed. "I was worried about the light, but we couldn't see where we were going without it. Can someone take Evangeline for a little bit? Be careful. Her ankle might be broken."

"They don't call me Big Dutch for nothing. I have broad shoulders." Luke passed his flashlight to Jace and seconds later the injured twin was tucked securely onto Luke's back.

Coral straightened, rubbed her lower back, and groaned.

"Are you okay?" Jace grasped her shoulder and she winced. "I'm sorry. Are you injured?"

Coral bit her bottom lip. "I'm good. Nothing to worry about." Goosebumps raced up and down her spine as an odd feeling settled over her suddenly. "We need to get out of here as quickly as possible. The suspect is armed with a rifle, and I'm sure all this ruckus we've created will alert him to our location."

"Agreed." Jace let go of her. "I don't think we're far from the road. We'll follow our steps back the way we came. Let's keep our conversation to a minimum." He held out his hand and lowered his voice. "Pass me your green light, Evangeline. At least it's not as bright as our flashlights."

A loud blast sliced the air nearby and Coral grabbed Jace's arm. "He's found us."

Before anyone could react, another shot rang out, followed immediately by crashing, thumping, and a scream. Coral's mouth went completely dry. Had one of them been hit? Jace's light flashed around the group, and her heart stopped at the awful scene. Luke was slumped on his side on the ground. Evangeline was down too, trapped beneath him.

Gabby shrieked. "My sister. Help my sister."

Coral dropped to her knees. Her stomach lurched at the blood on the officer's neck. "Luke's been shot. Hold on Evangeline. Jace, I need your help."

Jace knelt and lifted Luke's body enough to free the terrified twin from under the officer's dead weight. While Evangeline hobbled to her feet, seemingly unscathed by the bullet, Coral stared in horror at the geyser of blood spewing from Luke's neck. "No! No! No!" She whipped off her jacket, scrunched it into a ball, and applied pressure to the wound. "Hang in there, Luke."

Another shot rang out.

"Everyone get down and stay down," Jace barked.

The twins dropped to the ground and lay completely still.

"Nobody move. I'm going to try and find our shooter." Jace catapulted to his feet and disappeared into the woods.

Coral pressed on the leaking carotid artery with all the strength she had. *Please, God, don't let Luke die, protect Jace, and keep all of us safe.*

The air rang out with gunfire and it wasn't far away. "Stay flat on the ground, girls." Coral crouched as low as possible but continued the pressure on Luke's neck. She checked for a pulse. Faint but steady. *Dear God, please don't let him die.*

More shots. Then silence. Dead silence. Coral swallowed hard. Soft whimpers came from one of the twins. Coral listened intently, afraid to breathe as footsteps crunched behind her. Who had survived the gunfight? *Please God, let it be Jace.*

A bright light shone on Luke before a man knelt beside her. "How's he doing?"

"Jace. Thank God you're okay. Did you get him?" Coral's eyes were fearful yet hopeful as she tore her gaze from Luke.

"Got off a gunshot wound to his upper thigh. He's down about a dozen feet away, passed out cold. He's not going anywhere. He's handcuffed and I have his weapon. Calling for two ambulances. Give me a sec." Jace got to his feet, his worried features lit up by his screen's device. Coral couldn't make out what he said, but in thirty seconds he dropped beside her again. "They're on their way. They'll follow the GPS coordinates on my phone. How is he?"

"Not good. Unconscious and his pulse is faint. I'm pressing as hard as I can." Coral's voice broke. "He can't die. He can't. He just can't."

The twins were sitting up now, arms wrapped around each other as the girls cried softly. Coral wished with all her heart this hadn't happened to them, or to her, but mostly to Luke. He was such a good, kind man. He stood for all that was right in the world. *Why did he have to get shot, God? Why?*

Tears threatened, but she denied them, biting down hard on her trembling bottom lip. Now was not the time. She had to be strong for everyone, but mainly for Luke. It would take at least half an hour for the paramedics to get here. Did Luke have that long? A tight knot formed in her belly at the stark reality. She highly doubted it.

Please, God. I can't lose him.

Jace had wandered away for a few seconds then returned and was squatting at her side again. "The suspect is half-in and half-out of consciousness, ranting incoherently ... something about God getting him." He covered her shaking, bloodied, hand with his. "I've called it in to the station. Kensington is on his way. Let me press for a while."

Although Coral should have found consolation that God had indeed allowed the kidnapper to be caught, peace was elusive. Sure, the twins were safe, but Luke's life hung in the balance because of this evil man. "No. I'm okay."

"Let's all pray." Jace bowed his head. The girls' cries diminished to whimpers and sniffles. "Dear God, Luke Degroot is a good man. Please heal that blown artery and stop the bleeding." His voice hitched. "We need a miracle here."

Luke moaned. Jace shone the flashlight on his face.

"He's coming around," Coral exclaimed. Dare she hope he would be okay?

"Luke? Can you hear me?" Jace leaned in closer. Luke's nod was almost imperceptible. "Help is on the way. Hang on, buddy."

Coral lost her battle with restraint and tears streamed down her cheeks. "Luke, I have something important to tell you." Jace flung a glance at her, his brow wrinkled as if he sensed what was coming. Luke coughed, but it sounded more like a fluid-filled gurgle. He was choking on his own blood and his breaths were laboured.

"I love you, Luke Degroot. Don't leave me," Coral wailed. She leaned down and kissed his cheek.

"Did you hear that, Big Dutch? You've won. You are the best man." Jace's voice cracked.

Her eyes locked on Jace's shimmering ones before settling on Luke again. Despite the unfolding crisis, Coral's heart swelled at the sacrifice the man was making. She knew that, without a doubt, she'd made the right choice.

Luke's eyelids fluttered open and a weak smile crossed his face. "I won?"

"Yes." Coral stroked his cheek.

His eyelids closed. And the light went out of him.

A cry escaped her. "No. No. No." She pressed all the harder on his neck.

Jace hung his head. The twins were weeping. Luke was gone. She didn't know how long she pressed on his wound before Jace removed her hands. "He's no longer with us, honey."

Bright red lights flashed through the trees. Ironically, they weren't that far from safety after all. She heard voices, lots of voices, but was unable to move or respond—trapped in a horrific nightmare. Was this all a really bad dream caused by those chronic migraines? Oh, how she wished it were so.

Trapped in a fog, she heard Kensington speak as though from a long way off, urging the Fillmore twins to follow Officer Rodney Newton through the bush to the safety of a police cruiser. Loud yells cut the air, dragging Coral from her grief-filled cloud. Kensington placed a hand on her shoulder. "It's only the suspect yelling at the paramedics."

An inner urging prompted her. "I want to say something to Mr. Winkles."

"Are you sure? You're not thinking clearly right now, Coral."

"Yes. I need to do this." She struggled to her feet. Kensington wrapped an arm around her shoulders, and she was thankful for his support. Her knees wobbled and her strength waned, but she moved through the bush toward the injured, bound man.

Jace aimed a flashlight at the scene while paramedics worked to stabilize the kidnapper before loading him onto the stretcher.

"Don't touch me. You're making the pain worse. If I had my weapon right about now, you'd both be goners," Percy hollered at the paramedics. One was attempting to wrap the gunshot wound on his thigh, while the other was starting an IV drip.

Coral stepped closer. "Percy, can you hear me? It's Coral."

"I hear you all right. I didn't get shot in the ear. What do you want?"

"I ... I ... wanted to tell you that I forgive you." Her voice cracked as she choked back tears. Fingers squeezed hers and she realized they were Jace's.

"Ain't that wonderful. You forgive me. Now I can die in peace." His words dripped with sarcasm.

"No, you can't die in peace. Not until you confess your sins before God. You kidnapped two women and killed a police officer. There's not much hope that you'll ever get to see those daughters of yours again. Not after what you did."

Percy cried out in pain as they loaded him onto the stretcher. "I told you God hated me—that no one has ever loved me."

"No, God doesn't hate you. He hates what you did, but he will forgive you if you ask."

"Shut up, woman. I want no part of God. Not now. And not ever."

"We need to go," one of the paramedics urged.

Jace tugged at her hand. "Come on, Coral. Let him go. You tried." He led her through the trees toward the flashing lights of the cruiser, but she resisted, dragging him over to Luke's prone body. Two more paramedics were preparing to move him.

One last look at her fallen friend and she slumped to the ground. Jace dropped down beside her and pulled her into his arms. Coral collapsed against him, clinging tightly. Life would never be the same. Not ever again.

CHAPTER 25

Second Chances

Coral couldn't sleep. She couldn't eat. She couldn't focus. It had been almost a month since Luke's death, and nothing seemed right with the world. Jace had held her hand through the graveside service—a quiet rock of strength for her. Afterward, he'd tried to contact her a few times, even showed up at her door, but she didn't want to see him—or anyone—right now. Her bakery had remained closed since that dreadful day, and she had no immediate desire to reopen yet ... if ever. She thought back to the number of times her bakery had been closed for one reason or another since she opened last April. It was a miracle Coral's Muffin Cup Café had stayed afloat.

She needed this time to heal. To reflect. To grieve. Luke's senseless death made her angry. Angry with Percy Winkles. Angry with God. Even angry with herself. If she hadn't traipsed off in homicide detective mode to rescue the twins, things might have turned out differently. She should have listened to Luke and stayed in the kitchen.

But would things be different? Percy might have fled with the women and Evangeline and Gabby would never have been found. Who knew what kind of a life the Fillmore twins would have had to endure with this demented man? And think of the heartache to their parents if their daughters had never been found. Luke's job came with risk—high risk—but he had always felt called to serve the community in this capacity, even after his father had wanted his only son to take over the family farm.

Coral rose from the bench she'd been sitting on and ambled slowly along, her boots crunching on the fresh layer of snow that coated the lakefront path. Her breath puffed in front of her face, signifying the bitter cold the area was experiencing. January had come in with a frigid fury. She was ever so glad that she'd finally purchased appropriate clothing, footwear, and a shovel for life in this snowbelt region of Ontario.

If she truly believed that God was the giver and taker of life then she had to trust that this was in God's plan for Luke. Sad as it was. Her frantic prayer a month ago flashed through her thoughts—the prayer that God would help her conflicted heart, a heart torn between Luke and Jace's love. Was this the way God answered? By taking away one of them for good?

Staring heavenward, tears brimmed in her eyes again. Denying them, she blinked and squinted across the lake at the sun's waning brilliance as it dipped toward the horizon. In her heart of hearts, she knew God didn't work that way. Besides, before the unfolding events that day in the woods, she'd come to peace with her decision between Luke and Jace. Deep inside, Coral had known all along.

She blinked, unable to believe what she was seeing. As the sun hit the line between sky and lake, mini rainbows appeared on either side of the brilliant ball. She gasped, having never seen anything like it in her entire life.

"It's a sundog." The man's voice from behind her was so unexpected that it startled her, and she jumped.

"I'm sorry. I didn't meant to scare you." Kensington's apology came with a bashful smile and a shrug.

Coral blew out a breath. "It's okay. I didn't think anyone else was out on such a bitter cold day. A sundog you say?"

"Yes. It's a scientific occurrence when temperatures are extremely frigid like they are right now. Sundogs form when ice crystals are suspended in the atmosphere. Don't ask me to explain it in any more detail, but whenever I see a sundog I am reminded that even when life seems the coldest and harshest, God is here right in our midst, blowing us away with His beauty."

A healing balm coated her heart as the man spoke, and she knew without a doubt that his appearance had been a divine appointment. "I've never seen one before. God has shown me so many things since I moved here. I cannot doubt this was His plan all along, despite the loss of …"

A hand touched her shoulder. "How are you doing, Coral? I've been worried about you. Jace has been worried about you. In fact, many of us have been very concerned."

Coral swallowed against the thickening in her throat. "I'm … I've … not been good." Her eyes misted over again.

"I know you and Luke were close." He squeezed her shoulder before dropping his hand.

"We were." Instead of the heaviness that had been her companion through the last several weeks, something new was happening. *He restores my soul.* The verse from Psalms whispered in her heart, lifting her higher than the spectacle on the horizon. Coral knew that, for as long as she lived, she'd never forget this moment. The combination of the sundog and the verse left her with an unexplainable peace—one she had never felt before.

The older man smiled. "I had no idea I would find you down here today, Coral. I was out for a walk, filling time before I have to pick up Sylvia from her aunt's." He glanced at his watch. "Speaking of that, I'd better get going." He took a step to leave then stopped.

"This may be none of my business, and you can stop me if I'm overstepping my bounds, but there's a young man waiting to hear from you. In fact, I've never seen him so downtrodden. Please let him know that you're okay. He's beside himself with worry."

Coral's heart grew heavy. She hadn't thought of how her silence might be affecting anyone else–she'd been focused solely on her own grief. "You're right, I'll talk to Jace."

"Oh, and one more thing. I'd be honoured if you'd join me tomorrow night at my retirement party at the Elora Hall. I'll save you a seat at my table. I won't take no for an answer."

"Fine. Thank you. I'll be there."

After Kensington left, Coral studied the sundog again, completely in awe of its glorious, dazzling display. *He restores my soul.* Her peace deepened. Could someone burst with God's presence?

Unable to move, she realized that God was doing exactly that—restoring her soul. She watched the sundog until it disappeared into the twilight. Closing her eyes, she thanked God for bringing her here to Lighthouse Landing. Through all the heartache and grief, her walk with God had grown precious and sweet. She knew without a doubt that she'd never be able to stop singing His praises.

As Coral strode home to her apartment, an urgent mission charged through her. Two urgent missions, in fact. Hopefully, she wouldn't be too late. On either account.

After checking with Kensington to make sure Percy Winkles was still in the local hospital and that she'd be allowed to visit, Coral contacted the switchboard for the room number. Her heart pounded in her chest as the elevator stopped at the third floor. Could she do this? *Please God, give me strength.*

The doors slid open and she walked out. A policeman guarded a door at the far end of the hallway. Even from this distance, she knew by the size who it was. She felt Officer Rodney Newton's stink eye as he viewed her approach. Sheesh! He knew she was coming. What was all this about?

"I have permission to visit Mr. Winkles." Coral tipped back her head to meet the gigantic officer's wary gaze as he blocked the doorway. She wasn't short by any means at five feet, eight inches, but Newton's size dwarfed hers. Puzzled by his immovable, boulder-like stance, she tried to push past him, but he refused to budge. "Excuse me? Why are you blocking my entrance?"

"What is the nature of your visit with this murderer?" His cavernous voice ricocheted along the quiet corridor.

"I don't think that's any of your business. I have permission to see him, and that's all you need to know." She lifted her chin. She had never trusted this officer and apparently he didn't trust her either.

"Fine, but I'll be watching and listening." Newton stared down at her, his arms folded across his vest and his legs spread-eagled.

"Why? Do you think I'm going to spring him loose or something?" Coral quirked an eyebrow. Then another thought crossed her mind. Perhaps Newton thought she would try and kill the man for taking Luke's life.

"For your safety. After all, you're a civilian and that man is a kidnapper and murderer. What if he tries to hurt you?" His eyes softened slightly.

Oh. Okay. When he put it that way, she kind of understood his protectiveness. Officer Newton had a weird way of expressing himself. He finally stepped aside and allowed her entrance to the darkened room. The drapes were drawn, and machines beeped. A heaviness hung in the air, along with a pungent antiseptic smell. *Do you really want me to do this, God? Because you can stop me at any time.* Silence.

"Mr. Winkles?" Coral spoke softly so as to not alarm the sleeping patient.

An odd crackling sound accompanied each of his breaths. That didn't sound normal.

"Percy?" She raised her voice.

A coughing-wheezing noise reached her ears before he spoke. "Who's there? What do you want?"

"It's Coral Prescott. May I speak with you for a few minutes?" Slowly, she moved to the side of his bed. His sleepy eyes narrowed.

"What could you possibly want? And turn on the light so I can see what you're up to." His snarky command did little to ease her angst. What in the world was she doing here? But she knew. God had laid Mr. Winkles on her heart.

She reached up and pulled the chain behind his bed, illuminating the frail-looking forty-year-old man. Officer Newton's watchful gaze zeroed in on her as he leaned against the doorframe, half-in and half-out of the room.

"How are you feeling?"

"How do you think? As well as can be expected after being shot in the thigh." A rasping wheeze came from his chest, and he paused a moment before continuing. "Then those incompetent nurses let my wound get infected. As if that wasn't bad enough, I caught pneumonia. That's why I'm still here." Congested coughs wracked his body. "I'd rather be in prison than feeling like this."

"Well, that's why I'm here. That day in the woods—the day you shot Luke—I said I forgave you."

"Yeah, I remember. Very big of you."

"At the time, I felt strongly I needed to say them, but the words were meaningless. I see that now." Coral paused as beads of sweat broke out on her forehead. "I've spent the last month angry. I loved Luke Degroot and you took him away from me. However, I've come to realize that it was Luke's time to go. I miss him terribly, but because he had faith in Jesus, he's in heaven, no longer in pain, and visiting with his earthly and Heavenly Father. And I'm here today because Jesus loves you, Percy. He's willing to forgive you if you sincerely ask him. Jesus died on the cross for your sins—for the sins of all mankind. And unless you believe in your heart that you're a sinner and confess your sins before God, you will spend eternity in hell, apart from God."

Newton coughed in the doorway and shifted from one foot to the other. A sudden tormented wail caused Coral's heart to freeze. Percy Winkles was sobbing aloud. His reaction was so unexpected that she was rendered speechless. Officer Newton tilted his head, his forehead wrinkling in confusion. The patient's sobs carried terror, and Coral wasn't sure what to do. "Help me." Percy's one arm, free from an IV, flailed in the air before he flung it across his forehead.

"Are you in pain? Do you want me to get a nurse?" Coral moved closer to the side of his bed.

"No nurse. I'm in torment, but it's not physical. It's mental. I didn't mean to kill him. I really didn't. I've never killed anyone in my life before that policeman. I panicked and fired into the air. I was only trying to scare you all away so I could have my girls. I may be a lot of things, but I'm not a murderer. At least, I wasn't." He hiccoughed. "Will you forgive me? I didn't mean to kill that cop. I thought my shot went high into the trees. I'm really, really sorry."

Coral pressed her lips tightly together to stifle the emotions that threatened to come charging back as she remembered that painful scene in the woods. She swiped at a renegade tear. "I forgive you. And I truly mean it. I know you were desperate to keep your daughters."

"Thank you," Percy whimpered. "But now I need your help even more. Ever since that prison pastor started praying for me, God has been pursuing me like a hound after a rabbit. Day and night I'm tormented with visions of hell and it terrifies me. It could be the pain meds causing it, but I don't think so. How can I get God off my back?"

Coral smiled. "There's only one way, Mr. Winkles. Jesus is the Way, the Truth, and the Life. No man gets to heaven without believing that Jesus took your sins, my sins, the whole world's sins, upon His back on the cross in order to make a way for us to be with God forever in eternity. Do you believe that Jesus did that for you? Did you know He's pursuing you because He loves you? In fact, He sent me here today for that very purpose."

Percy was quiet. His eyes were closed. Newton stared at his feet and a thought crossed Coral's mind. Perhaps God had a two-fold mission for her today. Did Newton need to hear of Jesus' love too?

"I'm tired of running. I know I've messed up a lot in my life. But life's been so unfair to me. My parents were unfit, so I was taken from them at a young age and bounced around foster homes. To be honest, most of them were not much better." He paused as coughs shook his frame. "Then a high school romance led to a pregnancy with twins who were taken away from me. And Bethany, their mother, left me too. I've been wandering my whole life, feeling unloved." His voice cracked and a whistling wheeze filled the air. "That's why I had to have my daughters when I found them. I truly believe God led me to them. Don't you?"

Coral's heart softened as she gripped the top of the bed rail. "I'm so sorry for what you've been through. God may have allowed you to find your girls, but I'm sure He didn't lead you to kidnap them and murder a cop in the process. Are you ready to stop running?"

"I am. I'm sorry for everything. I want to change and be a different man. How do I accept this love of Jesus?"

Coral heard shuffling at the doorway and glanced over to see Newton backing into the hallway, a huge scowl on his face. She shifted her attention to the patient. "It's a simple but honest prayer from your heart. If you confess with your mouth that Jesus is Lord and believe in your heart that God raised Him from the grave, you will be saved."

Percy's eyes were still closed. "I believe."

A few minutes later, after promising to get Percy a Bible, she left his room. Newton refused to meet her gaze, instead seemed to be studying a design in the floor tile. Oh well. If she had made him uncomfortable, that wasn't her intent. Maybe something she'd said to Percy would get through to Newton, too. She'd leave that in God's hands.

Joy filled her heart as she made her way to the elevator. As horrible as the kidnappings and Luke's death had been, God was bringing good out of them, and she could not be more grateful for that.

CHAPTER 26

Class Clown and Hot-air Balloons

Sergeant Kelly stared at the computer screen in front of him, unable to concentrate on the report. After a few more minutes, he gave up with a loud exhalation of breath, closed the laptop, and lumbered to his feet. "What's the use?" He raked a hand through his hair and paced the small office as his mind rehashed the events of the last few weeks. No matter how many times he did, he always arrived at the same conclusion. Why was life so unfair? And why didn't God answer his prayers? He must be doing something wrong. He'd been certain God had prompted him to apply for Kensington's job. Now that he had it, but he didn't have Coral, he was confused. Didn't both go together? Did God place him here for another reason entirely? He had to admit he was slowly falling in love with life in this scenic locale, despite the brutal winters.

Sadness weighed heavily on his chest, making it hard to breathe. He remembered his desperate plea to God in the woods to save Luke's life. But it didn't happen. Why didn't God heal sometimes? He shook his head, unable to understand.

The community had come out in droves to pay their respects to Officer Luke Degroot after the loss of one of the town's finest. He'd been well-known and loved by many. With everything that had occurred in Lighthouse Landing over the last six months, evil seemed to be winning.

Hopefully, justice would be served against Percy Winkles, the man who'd abducted the Fillmore twins and murdered Officer Degroot. The accused was recovering from his bullet wound and awaiting trial. Oddly enough, he truly was the biological father of the twins. Jace figured that there would be a lot of healing needed in Gabby and Evangeline's lives—healing to recover from the trauma of the abduction and the truth of their heritage.

Why should Percy live while an innocent officer had lost his life?

The pressure on his chest increased as he remembered that he hadn't seen or heard from Coral since the funeral. Even Christmas and New Year's had passed quietly. Had the personalized snow-globe he'd given her not convinced her of his love? He desperately needed to know how she was holding up but wanted to give her space. Time to heal. After all, she'd loved Luke Degroot. A knot formed in his stomach and for the millionth time he wondered why he was still here in Lighthouse Landing. Jace's heart belonged to Coral, but she'd rejected him. What had happened between them? He had been so certain that she'd loved him too. He knew he'd never love anyone else.

It was Friday evening and quitting time. He turned off the lights to his office and locked the door. Tonight was Kensington's retirement party. Jace really didn't have any desire to go. He'd been depressed since Luke died. Not that he'd been that close to the man, but he liked him, and it was always sad when a fellow officer lost his life, especially in the line of duty. An even bigger source of his sadness was rooted in the reality that Coral didn't love him. She'd loved Luke.

He sighed and headed to his apartment, showered, shaved, and donned his best suit. It was his place to attend the retirement for a respected and honoured police sergeant. It would seem improper not to go. To be honest, he'd rather sit around in his underwear, put on an action movie, and stuff his face with pizza and chips—a habit he'd developed almost every night since Luke died. He'd already gained five pounds. If he wasn't careful, it'd soon be twenty-five.

After leaving his apartment, he drove to the edge of town and parked at the exclusive club. Inside the building, he followed the signs that led him to the event at the end of the hall. Soft music floated through the air and dim lighting created a warm atmosphere. Crowds of people mingled. Some were seated, some standing and chatting.

A hand waved through the air in his direction. It was Kensington at a table at the front of the room. Jace nodded and approached.

"Join us, Kelly. We saved you a place."

"Thanks. Which spot is mine?" Jace scanned the table that held seating for eight people. Immediately to Kensington's left sat his pretty wife, Sylvia, dressed in a gorgeous lilac gown. A dainty silver clutch sat on the chair immediately to her left. Then a seat sat empty. Next to that were the new mayor and his wife, Chris and Paula Robbins. They were in a deep conversation with the people seated beside them, Annie and Ernie Burwell, the wealthy couple who ran the Lighthouse Landing museum. They were the parents of Ryan Burwell, who had been arrested for his part in drug trafficking with the former mayor.

Kensington cleared his throat. "Take that seat on the other side of …"

Jace could barely stop his jaw from dropping at the sight of the woman approaching, a glass of punch in her hand. Coral had never looked more beautiful. Her dazzling, knee-length black dress shimmered with every step and clung to her curves as if the dress had been designed specially for her. Her dark, silky hair was up in some sort of bun, with wispy curls that dangled on either side of her face. A silver chain hung above a modest neckline, revealing the tiniest hint of her womanly attributes. Glimmering diamond earrings sparkled in her ears. Mercy. How would he survive the night seated next to her?

His heart raced erratically, then threatened to stall at the memory. She'd rejected him. He'd lost to Degroot. His head knew the horrific truth, but how did he convince his heart to accept it?

Their eyes connected and she stopped suddenly, her drink sloshing over her fingers. For an awkward moment no one else existed in that room but her. Drowning in desire for the woman who still held his heart, he couldn't look away. What a wretched dilemma!

Kensington cackled. "Sit down, Kelly. Your tongue is hanging out."

Heat crawled up Jace's neck and into his face. Normally, he didn't blush. Was his attraction to the woman that obvious? Jace hoped no one else had heard Kensington's embarrassing taunt. But he knew Coral had. He hurried to her side, reached for a napkin, and dabbed at her wet fingers.

"Thank you." Her voice was as sweet as a house wren's song—her cheeks also flushed with a rosy hue. When she smiled, he thought he'd go into full cardiac arrest. *Stop staring, Kelly or Kensington's going to embarrass you again.*

"Coral. How are you? You look absolutely incredible tonight. Happy belated Christmas and New Year's." Did he just say that? What a fool! He wet his lips, reached for the pitcher of water, and poured himself a glass.

"Same to you." Coral laughed softly as she set her glass on the table.

Jace pulled out the chair for her. He could fry an egg on his cheeks about now.

"Thank you." Her full pink lips mesmerized him as they turned up at the corners.

Jace chanced a look Kensington's way. Bad idea. His former boss was nailing him with an all-knowing grin. Oh boy. How could Kensington read him so well?

The emcee's voice hung somewhere in the background, but Jace couldn't make sense of the man's words—his radar was solely aimed at the stunning woman beside him. He reached for his glass of water and downed it, knowing full well he was in over his head. Her nearness left him struggling to think clearly, his thoughts bouncing helter-skelter all over the place. How would he ever get through the evening?

Kensington held the microphone in his hand. How did he get on stage? At first he spoke of his early years with the detachment and regaled the crowd with amusing stories. Then he grew serious as he talked of the recent loss of Officer Luke Degroot. Coral pulled a tissue from her clutch and dabbed at her eyes.

"And now I'd like to introduce my replacement, Sergeant Jace Kelly."

Jace dropped the dessert fork he was holding, and it clanged onto his plate. What? He didn't realize Kensington was going to do that.

"Could you stand please? Don't be shy, Kelly," Kensington implored him, lifting a palm in the air.

Okay. He wiped his mouth with his napkin, shot to his feet, and nodded at the crowd.

"Now, Sergeant Kelly will grace us with a few words."

What? Jace's mouth went completely dry. Was he supposed to have prepared a speech? Yikes. What in the world would he say? Public speaking had never bothered him; in fact he usually enjoyed the opportunity to be the centre of attention. But the crux of the matter was that he wasn't prepared.

"Come on up." The older sergeant waved a hand his direction. "We won't bite."

"You can do it." Coral touched his arm.

That was all the encouragement he needed. He hurried toward the stage and promptly tripped over an electrical cord near the bottom step. He stumbled and landed on one knee. Great. A few snickers rippled across the room as he limped up the steps.

Kensington clapped him on the back and handed him the microphone. "All yours, Kelly. Reel them in," his previous sergeant whispered as he made his way off the small wooden platform.

Jace stared across the audience. With all eyes on him, his goofy side took over. He never turned down the opportunity to be in the limelight. "Thanks a lot, Sergeant Kensington, for not giving me the heads-up that I was giving a speech tonight and for ambushing me with that cord. Do I detect a setup?" He chuckled and rubbed his knee. The crowd laughed with him. Jace's eyes flitted across the room. "And the sergeant doesn't have a clue what he did by handing me this microphone." He glanced at Kensington. "Did you know I was voted class clown in high school?"

More laughter.

"I promise I won't make my officers wear big red noses on the job."

Snickers and chuckles hung in the air.

"To be truthful, I'm not up to my class-clown self much lately." He felt Coral's eyes on him. "This community has been hard hit the last six months." Several heads bobbed in agreement. Emotion rose inside him that he hadn't expected. "I had the privilege of accompanying Officer Luke Degroot, or as he was affectionately known on the force, Big Dutch, that fateful day. Everything about him," his voice broke, "spoke dedication and bravery on the job. He lost his life saving the Fillmore Twins. Our community will forever be grateful for his sacrifice. I only wish I'd had the privilege of knowing him longer."

Silence reigned, which was good with him. He took the moment to collect himself.

"But seriously, I'm honoured to have been accepted for this position and to follow in such a great man's footsteps. From the short time I've known Sergeant Kensington, I have experienced a man that garners respect from everyone he comes in contact with. I only hope that I can live up to such high standards of integrity and fairness. I promise to give one hundred and fifty percent in hopes of being able to follow this remarkable man's legacy. Thank you, Sergeant Kensington. You're going to be a tough act to follow. I can only hope I don't trip and fall flat on my face. Can we hear it for Sergeant Kensington?" Jace set down the mike and clapped.

Not only did applause break out, people rose all over the room. They were giving their former police sergeant a standing ovation. Kensington's shoulders slumped forward, and he hung his head shyly before looking up again, a grateful yet bashful smile on his face.

Jace was stunned at the humility of the man. He sincerely hoped that one day he would develop such fine characteristics. Words from Coral's apology several weeks ago sailed through his thoughts—*God opposes the proud but gives grace to the humble.* He knew he had a lot to learn yet in this relationship with the God of the universe.

He returned to his seat as the emcee concluded the evening. Conversation resumed around the room as people mingled and chatted. A bolt of heat skittered across his shoulder. He looked over to find Coral's hand there.

"You did great. You're a natural in front of an audience." Her smile lit up his insides like fireworks on Canada's birthday, though the feelings charging through him were bittersweet. He thought of the promises he'd made to the community. It was almost as if he intended to stay. He did want to stay, didn't he? But how could he continue to see Coral and know that her heart didn't belong to him? That it had belonged to Luke.

"We need to talk."

Jace's eyes shot toward her. She wasn't smiling. Oh boy. His delicious prime rib dinner swirled and dropped like a punctured hot-air balloon. This was it. She was going to tell him to take a hike. That she no longer wanted him in her life. Which he'd kind of already suspected with her silence the last month.

"Let's go for a walk." Coral reached for the clutch purse at her feet. Jace stood and pulled back her chair. Kensington's inquisitive eyes met his, but the man didn't say a word. Jace followed her out of the event room and down a hallway to an inside courtyard, stopping before the statue of a young child. Water tumbled from a jug in the little girl's hand and collected in a pond below. Colourful fish swam in the swirling clear water and indoor plants surrounded the scene. The overall effect was pleasing to the eye—a direct clash with his turbulent emotions.

Coral sat on a nearby bench and patted the seat beside her. He loosened his necktie as he took his spot, being careful to keep a respectable distance for his own sanity. What was she going to say?

"How are you doing? Until your speech, I didn't realize that you thought that highly of Luke." Coral twisted the tissue in her hands.

"I'm okay. Oddly enough, the bond between us didn't really exist until that fateful day—the day he died. As we drove toward Thornton's Swamp, Degroot and I had a man-to-man talk about things. Mostly about you."

"Me?" Her pretty dark eyes twinkled with curiosity as her long lashes fluttered.

Jace swallowed. "At first, he vented his anger and frustration—anger over my absence from your life while he doted on you after your concussion at the hands of the town coroner. He never used the word doted, but I know that he faithfully cared for you. For that I will ever be thankful."

"He was very kind to me." Coral's voice trembled as she shredded her tissue with her fingers.

Angst filled him and he couldn't sit any longer. Jace shot to his feet, shoved his hands in his pants' pockets, and paced in front of the bench. "Did you know he'd given up? He mentioned that no matter what he did, you always kept him at arm's length. I encouraged him not to lose hope, and I guess I was right, although it pains me to say it."

A sob escaped her. She covered her mouth with a hand as her eyes grew glossy. "It's true that I kept him at arm's length."

"Obviously, something changed. Didn't I hear you tell Luke that you loved him right before he died? That the best man won?" His voice was quivering, but he didn't care.

Tears were trickling down her cheeks now. She swiped at them with the destroyed tissue in her hand. "You were the one who told him he'd won. I never said those words."

A flicker of hope ignited inside him. What was she saying? Coral got up from the bench, walked over to stand in front of him, and wrung her hands. "As I drove out to look for the Fillmore twins, I also did some soul-searching that day. That's when I came to a decision between the two of you."

Jace dropped his head and stared at the scuff marks on his freshly polished shoes. He knew what was coming. It hurt too much to drown in those incredible eyes any longer. "I know. You chose Luke. Please don't remind me. I've been in a tailspin of depression ever since. Did you drag me out here to the courtyard to make me relive the torture all over again? Because that's cruel. Frankly, I don't even know why I'm still in the community."

"You're not getting it. How dense can you be? I didn't choose Luke." She grabbed his shoulders and gently shook him.

Jace's head shot up so quickly he was sure he'd end up with whiplash. "Excuse me? I was there. Believe me, I heard you tell Luke you loved him. It almost killed me. How could I forget?"

Coral dropped her hands and swiped at her cheeks. "Of course I loved him. I loved him for the wonderful kind man he was. But the night he snapped at me and told me to keep out of the investigation and stay in the kitchen showed me a side of him I didn't like. I understand that I'm a civilian now and to be involved in police work would be dangerous, and perhaps he was only worried about me when he said it. But it was the way he said it. His words were nasty and cut very badly. I had considered his affections seriously until then, but how could I spend the rest of my life with a man who didn't trust me? Or believe in me?"

"We all make mistakes, Coral. I made the mistake of giving you the silent treatment for almost two months. Although I had my reasons, I hurt you and for that I'm truly sorry." Jace placed both hands on the top of his head. "Forgive me, but I must be really dense. I heard you tell Luke that you loved him, the night he was dying."

"I wanted to give him something to live for. I was hoping my words would help him hang on. And I truly did love him, just not in a romantic way. More like a brother or good friend. I knew he was dying, and I wanted to give him that last bit of hope to cling to. Can you fault me for that?"

Jace's heart leapt. "Wait a minute." His hands fell from his head and he held up his palms toward her. "You mean I didn't lose?"

"The night Luke was dying your words cemented my decision even more." She stepped closer and cupped the sides of his face.

He clasped her hands. "My words?"

"Yes. When I told Luke that I loved him, you congratulated your opponent and told him he was the best man and that he'd won. Despite the fact that you had misunderstood me, you accepted your defeat with such grace and kindness, although it must have pained you deeply. I knew then that I'd made the right decision. Luke had been a handsome distraction—but only a distant runner-up. I'd convinced myself I might have feelings for him because I was confused about us. It's always been you, Detective Jace Kelly. You were the reason I moved here in the first place. I needed to escape the pain of your rejection that day on the bridge in Sleepy Acres. Luke became a diversion from the agony in my heart."

He blinked. "You mean I won?"

Coral giggled. "You finally get it. I love you, Jace Kelly." On tiptoes, she brushed his lips with hers.

"What was that?" His voice rasped huskily. "I need a little more proof than that feathery glance from a butterfly's wings." Wrapping his arms around her waist, he pulled her close, dipped his head, and kissed her with a passion that had not only been building all evening but sent a tingle through him from head to toe. Salty and sweet all rolled into one, he lost himself in the essence of Coral. The kiss deepened and the cares of the world all fell away. He could stay here, in the moment, forever.

She broke the kiss, gasping for air. "Have mercy, Kelly."

"Sorry." He chuckled. Entranced, he stroked her hair and gazed into her alluring black eyes, his heart exploding with a love that was finally realized.

"Give me a second." She touched a finger to the end of his nose. Stepping out of his arms, she reached for the clutch she'd left on the bench and pulled out a small blue velvet box. His heart raced with wild recognition. Reaching for his hand, she placed the gift in his open palm. "Propose to me, Jace Kelly."

Jace threw back his head and laughed. And he laughed some more. Must be nerves. With trembling fingers, he opened the box, retrieved the ring, and dropped to a knee. "Coral Prescott. I love you with all my heart. I promise that I will always trust you, always love you, always stay true to you for as long as I live. Will you marry me?"

Coral held out her left hand and he slipped the ring onto her finger. "I've always loved you, Jace Kelly. And I always will. Yes. Yes. Yes, I will marry you."

"What are you doing on the floor, Kelly? Did you trip again?" Kensington's teasing voice boomed down the hallway.

"Jace proposed," Coral squealed, flinging her hand in the air.

Kensington walked toward them, clutching Sylvia's hand. He clapped Jace on the shoulder. "Congratulations. It's about time. I knew you two were meant to be together."

Jace shuffled to his feet, wrapped his arm around Coral's waist, and stared into her eyes. "From the moment I helped her up from her little tumble on the slippery rocks at Sleepy Acres Campground, I knew I was a goner."

"You mean the time you crushed your caboose?" Coral teased.

Kensington raised an eyebrow and smirked. "Crushed cabooses aside, can Sylvia and I impart a little matrimonial advice?"

"Please." Jace beamed.

"We'll cherish anything from a couple that has been married as long as the two of you," Coral added.

Kensington gazed at his wife—his eyes full of warmth. "These words from Micah 6:8 have been my motto since the day I married my sweetheart and they've served us well for forty years. What does the Lord require of you? To act justly, and love mercy, and walk humbly with your God." He pulled his wife into a hug. "If you do these things, your marriage will be blessed." Kensington tugged on his wife's hand. "And now we'll leave and give you two some privacy."

Jace's heart squeezed as he watched the older couple leave. What a beautiful bond between the two of them. God was definitely driving home humility with Jace today. With God's help he would continue to pursue justice in his role in law enforcement, seek mercy whenever he made a mistake, and love God, Coral, and others with all the humility he could muster.

Coral loved him, and they were going to get married. He pulled her close, joy galloping through him. "Tonight is so much better than lounging around in my skivvies, stuffing my face on pizza." He kissed her hair.

"Huh?" Coral's brow wrinkled as she looked up at him.

He kissed her nose. "Never mind, my little Coral Muffin Cup. Never mind at all."

BOOKS BY LD STAUTH

Campground Mystery Series

1. Stormy Lake
2. Lake of the Cross
3. Starry Lake

Lighthouse Landing Trilogy

1. Laugh in the Woods Turns Deadly
2. Lighthouse Landing Lament
3. Snowsqualls and Missing Elves

ABOUT THE AUTHOR

The desire of three-time award winning author LD Stauth's heart is to encourage her readers. An avid camper, she continually marvels at God's creation revealed in nature. Her husband of forty-five years, four children, and nine grandchildren bring her much joy, and sometimes fodder for her stories. In elementary school, LD won a poetry contest on why she loved Canada. It was published in a book called *Windsor's Budding Poets.* Since then writing was sporadic while raising her children. But that changed after a short story about her first grandchild, entered in a contest sponsored by The Word Guild, (a nationwide Canadian writing organization) won. That life-changing event opened the door to novel writing. It wasn't until 2017 when her first book went to publication. Since then all three novels in her *Campground Mystery Series* have won awards. Her books have been called fun and are filled with laughter, romance, mystery, and most of all hope.

To contact:

Facebook at https://www.facebook.com/ldstauth.8/
email at ldstauth@gmail.com
Website at https://www.ldstauth-author.com/

Made in the USA
Middletown, DE
21 November 2020